GIRL TWO: TAKEN

TAKEN

(A Maya Gray FBI Suspense Thriller—Book 2)

Molly Black

Molly Black

Debut author Molly Black is author of the MAYA GRAY FBI suspense thriller series, comprising six books (and counting); and the RYLIE WOLF FBI suspense thriller series, comprising three books (and counting).

An avid reader and lifelong fan of the mystery and thriller genres, Molly loves to hear from you, so please feel free to visit www.mollyblackauthor.com to learn more and stay in touch.

ISBN: 978-1-0943-9322-3

BOOKS BY MOLLY BLACK

MAYA GRAY FBI SUSPENSE THRILLER
GIRL ONE: MURDER (Book #1)
GIRL TWO: TAKEN (Book #2)
GIRL THREE: TRAPPED (Book #3)
GIRL FOUR: LURED (Book #4)
GIRL FIVE: BOUND (Book #5)
GIRL SIX: FORSAKEN (Book #6)

RYLIE WOLF FBI SUSPENSE THRILLER
FOUND YOU (Book #1)
CAUGHT YOU (Book #2)
SEE YOU (Book #3)

CHAPTER ONE

FBI Special Agent Maya Grey sat in the hospital and waited, hoping that soon she would get some answers. Just on the other side of the door, the woman she'd managed to save from a deadly kidnapper lay with doctors tending to her. Maya could feel her frustration rising at not being able to ask any questions until they were done. This woman held the answers. And every second mattered.

It had been days now since Maya had received the postcard that had claimed a kidnapper was holding women, and had signed off with the nickname that Megan had always used for her. Maya had to know if this man really had her sister, and *where*.

Maya tried to be patient. She was just one of the half dozen FBI agents waiting there. Maya could only guess at the ordeal the twenty-two-year-old singer had gone through.

"You'll get to talk to her soon," Marco Spinelli said. He had done so much to help her get this far, and Maya felt herself growing closer to him.

He'd stayed, even though Maya guessed that he should be getting back to his job as a Cleveland detective. He sat beside her, muscled swimmer's frame crammed into a hospital chair, so that for once he didn't tower over Maya, tall as she was. His dark hair was more tousled than usual, and those piercing gray-blue eyes seemed more tired than usual.

Maya knew how he felt.

"The doctors have told us nothing," Maya said. "We could be here an hour or a week."

"We have time now," Marco pointed out. "There's no deadline for *this* part."

No, the deadline had been for the last case, trying to solve it on the whim of a man who claimed to have kidnapped twelve women, twelve "bunnies," to be returned only if Maya did what he wanted.

Maya stood, stretching. As she did so, she caught a glimpse of herself reflected in the glass of Liza Carty's room. She looked a mess, with her dark hair escaping from its ponytail, her FBI standard suit

1

definitely in need of dry cleaning, her features looking their thirty five years and more now that she was tired. She normally didn't care about appearances, but in front of Marco, she had the urge to fix her hair, at least.

She was just beginning, when the alarms started to go off in the room beyond the glass.

A doctor came running out. "We need some help in here!"

"What's going on?" Maya asked, following him.

"She's crashing. I need to get back in there now, and you need to let me do my job!"

Maya let him go, watching as he and a couple of other doctors ran into the private room and started to work on Liza Carty. She saw one of them grab a needle from a crash cart, jabbing it into her while another started chest compressions. After that, though, one of the nurses drew the blinds on the room, making it impossible to see inside.

"What's going on here?"

Maya turned to see Deputy Director Harris approaching, along with most of the other agents there. A couple of them had their hands on their weapons, reacting as if the alarm meant some kind of attack. Maybe it was just because that was the kind of situation they could actually do something about, and it was better than just standing there waiting.

Harris stood there, looking serious in his expensive suit and with his closely shaved head. He fiddled with the gold clip of his tie. For once, he didn't look like someone's rich uncle, just her boss, serious and all business.

"We need her to catch this bastard, Grey."

He didn't have the incentive of trying to save Megan, but it was obvious by this point that he wanted to catch the kidnapper at least as much.

A doctor came out, looking serious but relieved.

"How is she?" Maya asked.

"Ms. Carty is back with us," the doctor said, "and has managed to wake up, but she is very weak. I don't want anyone disturbing her until she has rested fully."

"Doctor," Harris said. "Do you understand that this is a witness in a case where multiple lives are at stake?"

"The life I care most about at the moment is hers," the doctor said. "That was a very close call."

2

"I still don't think you understand the situation," Harris said.

"I understand that Ms. Carty is a very ill woman," the doctor replied. "From what I understand, she was subjected to a very traumatic experience, and the physical aspects of it have proved considerable."

"Will she recover?" Maya asked.

"We have no way of knowing at this stage," the doctor said, "and I can really only release more information to Ms. Carty's family."

"We are in the middle of a serious and urgent investigation," Harris said.

"And I am in the middle of trying to save my patient's life. Step aside, please, we need to get back to our jobs."

Maya and Harris had to move to one side to let out the remaining doctors and nurses from the room. Maya saw them going back to their other patients in the busy ER and felt a moment of appreciation for how difficult their jobs had to be, trying to save lives.

But she was too, and she couldn't just let this go. Nor, it seemed, could Harris.

"Doctor," he said, and now other agents started to group around him, near the door. "You're obstructing an active investigation, one in which the lives of another eleven women may be at stake."

He was using his most authoritative voice now, the one he saved for when he was in wrangles with other departments within the FBI, or when he had to make it clear to local cops that they had jurisdiction over a particular case. It was a voice that got people to back down, in most cases.

Finally, the doctor sighed.

"Make it quick," he said, conceding.

To Maya's surprise, Harris looked at her, and nodded to her, singling her out to talk to the patient.

Maya wasted no time. She slipped past them and stepped into the hospital room.

Liza Carty was sitting up on the bed, but she didn't look good. She was so pale she was almost gray, her blonde hair plastered with sweat. The tubes and wires connected to her didn't help either.

Even so, she managed a smile as Maya came in.

"Agent... Grey. Am I ok? The doctors won't tell me anything."

"How do you feel, Liza?" she asked in her most calming and compassionate voice.

3

She didn't have much time before a doctor came in, but even so, she knew that she had to do this gently.

"Like I've been hit by a truck. My chest feels so tight."

"Try not to think about it now," Maya said. She took a breath. "Liza, I need to ask you some questions about what happened to you. Anything you can tell me might help the others there. There *are* others there, right?"

"Eleven," Liza managed. "Eleven others. I…"

She trailed off, then she looked right at Maya, her eyes shining with intensity.

"I met your sister."

Maya's heart fell.

Those words confirmed all of her worst fears. They made her feel sick with worry, and fueled the need to know more. She *had* to find Megan and the others.

"Is she all right?" Maya needed to know that her sister wasn't hurt or worse. That there was still some chance to save her.

"She's there…" Liza said, "…he kept us all together, like…like….Megan and I tried to escape. That's when… that's when he chose me."

Was it just random, then? Maya had assumed that this had something to do with the victim in the last murder she'd investigated.

"Is everyone there a performer?" Maya asked, thinking of the theory that she and Marco had come up with when they'd found out about the possible link between Liza as a singer and the cold case victim, who'd been a dancer.

"I… don't know," Liza said.

"What about the man who held you?" Maya said. "Can you tell me anything about him?"

Liza started to shake her head.

"He wore a mask."

"What about his voice? His eyes? His hands?"

Maya would take any information she could get right then. Looking round, she could see Agent Ignatio Reyes peeking in at the door.

"He… he had a…bland voice," Liza said. "Except… he sang to me. That last night, he sang…I think he sang before…"

It wasn't much, but it was something. Maya kept going, and as she did so, she saw Agent Reyes in the doorway, listening in. Maya wasn't sure how she felt about that. Reyes was a good agent, and he wanted

4

the truth in all this as much as Maya did, but he'd already shown that he cared more about catching the kidnapper than about keeping her sister safe.

"What about the place you were held?" Maya asked. "What do you remember?"

Maya saw beads of sweat break out on Liza's face as she thought. She hated pushing Liza like this, but she needed to know. Not just for her sister's sake. But for those ten other women, too.

"There were…rooms…corridors…no windows. I think… I think maybe it was underground?" Liza didn't sound sure.

"What about when he took you out of there?" Maya said. "Did you get any glimpse of where it was?"

Again, Liza shook her head.

"He blindfolded me…told me he'd kill me if I…if I took it off."

"I understand," Maya said. There had to be something, though. Everyone made mistakes, no matter how careful they were. "How long did you drive to get where he dropped you?"

"Maybe…an hour?" Liza said.

A lot of places could be an hour from where they'd made the handoff.

"Is there anything else?" Maya asked. "Anything at all?"

Liza seemed to gaze off into space. Maya wondered how much of her was present, and how much was lost in nightmares. She hated questioning her in this state. But she also didn't want to see eleven more women die.

Or her sister.

"Please, Liza."

"Violets," she said. "I remember the smell of violets. Overwhelming, and it…"

She clutched a hand to her chest, and suddenly all the alarms were going off again.

"Doctor!" Maya called out, but the doctor was already rushing back inside.

"Get out!" he screamed.

He rushed over to Liza and Maya stumbled out, having to make way for the other medics who ran in even as she left.

She found herself standing outside, feeling awful.

Had she just pushed Liza too hard? Or was this going to happen anyway, and she'd just gotten the little she could in the time? The

5

thought of saving Liza only to lose her was too much. She slumped back against the wall, waiting, feeling guilty. She shouldn't have pushed like that, no matter the reason, even with lives at stake.

It was only a few minutes before the doctor came out again, with an angry expression on his face.

"I hope you got what you wanted, Director," he said bitterly to Harris, not bothering to hold back his anger, "because you just put my patient in danger. We got her back again, but *no one* else is to go in there. Do you understand?"

Maya winced at that. She'd done everything she could to save Liza, and now, she'd put her in more danger.

"I want you out of my ER," he said to Harris.

Harris glanced at Maya, who nodded back. She'd gotten all she could for now.

She needed to give Liza time to recover, and she felt sure that when she did, Liza would have much more to say.

In the meantime, Maya would save them, whatever it took. She would go back into work tomorrow, wait for the next postcard, and try to take it further.

For now, though, all she had to go on was the smell of violets.

CHAPTER TWO

Maya jogged, trying to push thoughts of the case from her mind. It was driving her mad, no postcard arriving to tell her what came next. All Maya knew was that there were still eleven women in danger, including her sister, and the one clue she had made no sense. What could she get from the smell of violets?

Maya would have to get in to work soon, so she ran back to her apartment to shower. She grabbed her mail as she came back in, quickly rifled through it, her heart pounding.

And then her throat went dry.

There it was. Right on schedule.

Another postcard.

Maya froze in place, looked around for any way that someone might be watching. The kidnapper couldn't just be sending these through the mail, could he? Not with the way they arrived so suddenly, out of nowhere.

There was no sign of anyone, though.

The card had the usual bunny motif on the front, a dozen of them hopping around a field. No, not a dozen, *eleven*. Even in that, the killer was playing games with her. Maya picked the card up by the corners, turning it over.

There were just five words on the card this time:

Please don't come for me.

Those words made Maya's blood run cold, not because of the words themselves, but because this wasn't the usual neat copperplate that the kidnapper favored. Instead, it was a sideways slanting scrawl that Maya knew from helping with homework and notes stuck to a fridge.

It was her sister's handwriting.

*

By the time Maya got to her department's offices on the fourth floor of the FBI building, there were already plenty of people there.

Harris was standing in front of a screen, with Reyes by his side, and ten or eleven other agents sitting around watching.

"This is the location," Deputy Director Harris said. "There are entrances here, here, and here. We believe that the suspect is most likely to be in this area, which appears to be the most easily defended."

Maya could see an overhead shot of a location on the screen, along with floorplans for a building she didn't know. It looked like some kind of factory. Maya instantly knew what they were doing there, because she'd sat in on more than enough meetings like this before.

They were planning a raid.

"Three tactical teams will strike simultaneously, taking the entrances at once, so that there's nowhere for him to run," Harris said. "We'll go in quietly this time, and we'll check for traps along the way."

It *could* have been for something else. Maybe Reyes had finally cracked that narco ring he'd been working on. Maybe one of their cases had turned up a spot where organized crime was stockpiling weapons or drugs. A part of Maya hoped that it was going to be one of those, but two things told her that it wasn't. The first was the look on Reyes's face as she walked in, caught between guilt and defiance, getting ready for an argument. The second was that, suddenly, everything her sister had been made to write on the postcard made sense.

"You think you've found the kidnapper, don't you?" Maya said.

Harris looked over to her, looking pleased.

"Reyes told us about the information you were able to get from Liza Carty before she passed," he said. "Well done, Grey."

"Well done?" Maya said. "All I got from her was the scent of violets."

"The *overwhelming* scent of violets," Reyes said, looking pleased with himself. "So I got to thinking, that's not just a garden or a bottle of perfume, is it? I started looking around at everywhere within an hour of where we picked up Ms. Carty, and I found this place."

"What is that place?" Maya asked.

"An abandoned factory for bath products. Large scale, used to supply half the big brands with their products before it became cheaper to just import them. If anywhere is going to smell of violets, it's there."

"And every florist, garden nursery, and bath product *store,*" Maya pointed out. She didn't like how quickly the others were jumping at this.

8

"But where would you keep twelve women in a place like that?" Harris said. "This factory is a perfect location for it. Someone could hide out there for years without anyone finding out. No, Grey, this is the spot."

"You need to cancel the raid," Maya said. In that moment, all she could think about was the danger to her sister. The kidnapper warned them last time they tried something like this. Did the others really think that he was going to keep it to a warning this time?

"Grey, we have a location," Reyes said. "I'm sure about it."

"And how did that go last time?" Maya asked. "When you went ahead with a raid and got three SWAT guys hurt?"

"Grey, my office, now!" Harris snapped, and it was only then that Maya realized that she'd gone too far with Reyes.

Still, at least alone, there might be a chance to persuade Harris to call this off before it all went bad.

Maya marched through to Harris's office, waiting for him to take his seat behind the expanse of his desk and shutting the door behind her.

"You can't talk to Reyes like that in front of the others," Harris said. "He's put real work into finding this location."

"Because of something he overheard from a hospital doorway," Maya said.

"Which I notice you didn't share, Grey."

"Like you didn't share the fact that you were building up to a raid?" Maya wasn't going to let go of that easily, not when her boss might be putting her sister in danger.

"After everything you've just been through, I was pretty sure you would need some time," Harris said.

Maya shook her head. "That's not the reason."

The pause that followed was uncomfortable, with her eyes locked on Harris's.

"All right, no," he said. "That's not the reason. Your closeness to this case motivates you to find answers, but it also means you can't make objective decisions about the best moves to make."

"Like organizing a raid based on Reyes's guesswork?" Maya still couldn't quite believe that everyone was so locked in on one specific location.

"Reyes is a good agent, and you know it. Why wouldn't I go along with a chance to end this?"

Maya took out the postcard that had been left in her mail and put it down on the desk for Harris to read.

"Because he knows you're coming."

She saw Harris pick it up, looking it over. She caught the surprise on his face at the message there.

"This isn't the same writing as the previous ones," Harris said. Maya was surprised that he picked up on that detail so quickly.

"It's my sister's writing," Maya said. "His way of reminding me that he has her, and that she's in danger if we try to catch him. We *can't* go through with this raid, sir."

"What are we meant to do?" Harris said. "Sit back and play his little game until he gets bored and kills the hostages anyway? Liza Carty died from the way he treated her, Grey."

Did he think Maya didn't know that? That she hadn't spent most of the night wondering what she might have done differently?

"We have to be the ones to end this," Harris said.

"This will just turn into a repeat of the raid on the apartment building," Maya countered.

Harris shook his head, though. "That was thrown together with local cops and a few agents from a field office. This will be us. We'll do it right."

Maya still wasn't convinced. "He avoided us at the handover. He's been several steps ahead of us the whole time. This could all just be another trap."

"You think he somehow faked all this?" Harris said. "No, at some point, we have to trust the information we get from his captives. He's warning us off to buy himself time to move them. We have to move now. Don't you *want* to catch him?"

"Of course I do," Maya said. "I want it more than you do. But I also don't want to take risks."

"So we won't take risks," Harris said. "We'll go in quietly, monitoring for electronic surveillance. No doors battered down, no explosions. He won't even see us coming."

Maya wished that she could believe that, but this was a man who seemed to be able to look in on every aspect of her life. He was *definitely* monitoring police radio channels.

"Sir," she began, determined to make one last attempt to convince him. "This will fail. He's seen it coming, and he'll be prepared. You're playing with the lives of eleven women."

"You're too close to this, Grey," Harris said. "This is happening, and soon. You have to decide if you're in or you're out. We'll do this right, but we *are* doing this."

Maya felt sick in that moment, not knowing what to do. She wanted to stop the raid, but she couldn't. She needed help, needed to talk to someone.

Right then, there was only one person who might understand.

CHAPTER THREE

Maya rushed out into the hallway, took out her phone, and called the number she had for Marco Spinelli. She felt herself let out a breath she hadn't realized she was holding when he answered at once.

"Maya, is everything ok?"

"Not even close," she said. Maybe she should have pretended, but it felt as though Marco was someone she didn't *have* to pretend with right now.

"What happened?" he asked.

Maya tried to put her thoughts into some kind of order. "Reyes thinks he worked out where the kidnapper is, again. Which means that Harris, our boss, is going all in on another raid."

"That's..."

"Stupid? Dangerous? Likely to get my sister killed?" Maya could think of plenty of other reasons why this was a bad idea, but that was the big one. The enormity of it was overwhelming, and the fear for Megan was enough to make her voice catch as she said it.

"They can't go in if they think there's a risk," Marco said.

"They think they've got it all figured out." Maya put a hand to her head, trying to forestall the headache that the tension was bringing on.

"And do they?"

"He knows they're coming, Marco," Maya said. "He made my sister send another of those postcards, telling me not to come for her. It's a threat, and they're *ignoring* it."

Which meant that Maya wasn't in control of the situation. She had to stand by, helplessly, while her colleagues put Megan in danger. She felt as though she was on the verge of breaking down, right then and there on the phone.

All of that, and it had been Marco she'd called. Marco, not her mother, not one of her colleagues. She'd called a Cleveland detective she'd worked with once over people she'd been working with for years, and had done it so automatically she hadn't even thought about it.

12

"This is still your case," Marco said. "They can't cut you out of it. There's a reason that the kidnapper has gotten in touch with *you*, not with them."

"Because they don't have sisters he can grab?" Maya suggested. She felt on the verge of panic, and she hated that, because she wasn't someone who panicked.

"That's not it and you know it," Marco insisted. "He needs something from you. You solved the Anne Postmartin case when no one else could have. He can't hurt your sister, or he won't get anything else from you."

Maya hoped that was true, but she'd also seen how ruthless the kidnapper could be.

"Just don't give up," Marco said. "And don't let them push you out of this. Maybe you can stop this. Even if you can't, you can at least be there to try to make sure things don't go bad. Don't give up on this, Maya."

He made it sound so simple, but Maya knew it was true. She had to keep trying to stop the raid; and if she couldn't do that, then at least she could *be* there for her sister. She could try to get to her before the kidnapper had a chance to hurt her.

She just had to hope that she would be able to save her. In that moment, Maya knew what she was going to do. She was going on the raid.

*

"Are you sure you should be here, Grey?" Harris asked, as Maya walked up to the staging point.

They were in the woods beyond a small town, with half a dozen FBI vehicles waiting in a clearing. Maya could see three tactical teams gathered, in full armored gear, with automatic weapons held ready. Maya could see Reyes off to one side, talking a couple of agents through the plans for the factory.

"I need to be here, sir," Maya said.

Harris shook his head. "You're too close to this."

"Do you think that will stop me from doing my job?" Maya countered. "This is still my case. I'm the one the kidnapper is in contact with. I'm the one who helped to *get* us to this point. I deserve to be here."

13

Harris looked as if he might argue, but was there anything there that he could really argue with? Maya had very carefully not mentioned her sister, even though the fear for her was eating her up inside.

"All right," he said. "When we get to the hostages, it will be good to have someone psychologically trained on the team."

When, not if. Harris was still treating this like a done deal. Still, Maya was grateful that she could at least be there, and play her part in this.

She took a few moments to look over at the former factory. It stood, rusting now above the line of the trees, gantries and walkways making it look as if someone had transplanted an oil rig into the middle of nowhere. The more Maya looked at it, the more convinced she was that this wasn't going to work.

"Show me the plans?" Maya said.

"You think you're going to spot something that the rest of us have missed?" Harris countered, but he showed them to her anyway.

Maya supplemented them by getting out her phone and calling up map views of the area. Zooming in until she could see every detail of the place.

How would she raid it if she were the one planning this? How would she defend it? It wasn't just Maya's FBI training that helped her there; her time in the military let her see all the lines where an oncoming force would be vulnerable to attack, and the places where they might be able to infiltrate.

She could see that Harris was right about there being only three main points of entry. That made it less likely that any suspect would escape, but it also made the location more defensible. It was the kind of place that she would have dreaded assaulting if there were dug-in insurgents, and Maya suspected that the only reason it was viable now was that there was only meant to be one man there.

The kidnapper had shown before, though, that he was more than capable of outwitting the FBI alone.

Maya contemplated the plans. Was it possible to defend a place like that alone? No, that was the wrong way of thinking about it, the way Harris, Reyes, and the rest were probably thinking about it. They saw a vast factory space and one man trying to hold off the full might of the FBI, but this wasn't about how long he could hold out. It was about the damage he could do.

14

Maya decided to assume for a moment that the kidnapper was there. After the raid on the apartment building, that was a big assumption, but maybe Reyes had this right. He was a good agent, and if he said this was the only place that matched the clue Maya had gained from Liza Carty, it was probably true.

So maybe this *was* the place, but that meant that they had to make the assault on the factory and get to the hostages before the kidnapper could, in a place that Maya had plenty of doubts about, tactically.

Her first was if they would be able to approach without being spotted. Looking at the maps, the factory was pretty far from anywhere else, maybe because of the volatile processes involved there. If they approached down the road, or by helicopter, it would be possible to see them coming from a mile or more away.

The images of the factory showed outside gantries around large tanks designed to hold chemicals. Any one of them could provide a vantage point. On another day, Maya might have worried about a sniper there, but now she was just worried about the possibility of the kidnapper being out there, checking for trouble, when they approached.

Her second big doubt was the doors. Ok, so Harris had said that they were going in quietly, but with an abandoned factory, would that even be possible? Out so far from anywhere, the doors wouldn't be dainty little apartment ones. They would be thick, solid things designed to deter thieves, and by this point, there was every chance that the locks would have rusted. Maya could imagine the noise it might make trying to get through them, and that was if there wasn't a camera pointed at every door as a relic of the factory's security system.

Which brought Maya to her third big concern: who they were going up against. The kidnapper had been ahead of them at every stage, and he hadn't shied away from using violence. What was to stop this from being another place riddled with traps and explosives? What was to stop this guy from seeing them coming, and killing his captives?

Killing Megan.

That was the biggest part of it. Maya stared at the plans, trying to find a way through the problems, trying to find a way that she could be sure that her sister would be safe, but the truth was that there were no guarantees with a plan like this. There was nothing she could do, and Maya *hated* feeling that helpless.

"There's no way to approach unobserved," she said.

15

"We know what we're doing, Grey," Harris said. "We're going through the trees right up to the fence line. The map is clear.

"The map isn't the territory," Maya insisted. "Look, you can see what a good view anyone on the top level would have of people approaching."

"Our snipers haven't spotted anyone so far," Harris said. "No movement."

Maya still wasn't ready to let it go. "Sir, I can't see a way to do this quietly, and if he hears us coming, we're risking the lives of the hostages."

"You think you know better than everyone on the FBI's tactical teams?" Harris replied. "They've assessed this, and the risk of collateral damage is well within acceptable operational limits."

"Acceptable operational limits?" Maya said. The hostages weren't an acceptable loss. Her *sister* wasn't an acceptable loss.

"We need to catch this guy, Grey," Harris said. "He's made us look stupid twice now, and I'm not going to let there be a third."

"Sir," Maya said. "I'm begging you, don't go through with this. Look at that place. Even if he's there, even if this isn't all another trick, it's a death trap!"

Harris gave her a hard look then. "This is why I didn't want to invite you along on this raid, Grey. We can't afford to have anyone along who isn't committed to this mission. Who'll hesitate. This is happening. The only thing you need to decide now is whether you're going to help, or whether you want to stay behind in the tactical van and watch the whole thing on camera."

There was a steeliness in his voice that made it clear that he wasn't going to back down. Harris moved away, going over to the tactical teams to give them their final briefing.

That left Maya alone, trying to make up her mind. She still wanted to find a way to stop this, but now it felt like trying to swim against a raging current, impossible to go against. All she could do now was go with it, try to steer things, and hope that she could do it in such a way that her sister didn't wind up dead.

Readying her gun, Maya moved forward to join the others.

CHAPTER FOUR

Maya advanced through the woods with her weapon drawn, certain all the time that she shouldn't be doing this. Other agents advanced around her, most wearing gas masks and tactical vests, many of them sporting weaponry better suited to a war zone than anything domestic.

Maya had a gas mask at her own belt, an earpiece in her ear and a tactical vest strapped on beneath her jacket, but she'd kept the weaponry down to just her Glock. At the kind of close quarters the factory promised, some of the long rifles a couple of the other agents sported might prove to be more of a liability than a boon.

"Radio check," Harris's voice said through the earpiece.

"Hearing you loud and clear," Maya said. She didn't try to argue against the mission now. There was no way that Harris was going to call it off, so the only hope was to go in and try to make sure that her sister came out of this alive.

They were getting closer now, with the bulk of the factory looming over them. Maya could see the anxiety on the faces of the other agents there, and guessed that her own face would look just as tense. It was never easy, in the moments before plunging forward into the unknown, not knowing what opposition they might face.

As they broke the tree line, they sprinted for the door they'd been assigned. Maya watched one specialist push an endoscope camera under the door to get a view inside, then pull back so that another could drill the lock. It was quick, but far noisier than Maya would have liked.

So much for going in silently.

"Masks on," Harris's voice said in her ear. Maya hurried to pull the gas mask into place. "Gas going inside in three, two, one. Go!"

One of the agents with her threw a cannister into the factory, and it hissed as CS teargas started to pour from it. The idea was that the kidnapper would be forced out by it, disoriented and dazed.

It also reduced visibility, but with torches slung under their guns, the agents started to force their way inside. Maya went with them, keeping a careful watch for any traps.

"Stop!" she called out, and the agent in front of her froze in place. Maya crouched, looking at the glint of a tripwire up close. Working very carefully, she reeled in the wire and replaced the arming pin in the claymore mine.

"We've got anti-personnel claymores here," she said. "Watch your step."

"Already found one," Reyes's voice came back. "Still think we're in the wrong place, Agent Grey?"

"There were mines in Pittsburg, too," Maya pointed out. A part of her was excited by their presence, though, because it meant that at least this place actually had something to do with the kidnapper.

That excitement was tempered by just how quiet everything was in the factory.

Maya started to pick her way through it, moving as quickly as she dared given the risk of mines. Her pistol swept the corners of the room they were in, where large vats stood in silent rows, just starting to emerge out of the gas. Walkways stood above, presumably to allow the people who had once worked there to adjust the mixes. A long conveyor belt looped around the space, broken towards one end.

Maya knew the plans of the place as well as anyone now, so she moved towards the doors leading to a suite of labs and offices. The other agents went with her, and for once, Maya was grateful for other people around her. It meant that, between them, they could cover all the angles.

Going to the first office, Maya stepped up next to the door and waited for the others to stack up behind her. Taking a step back, she started to open it, then stopped as she saw another wire glittering just beyond the door.

"No one is to kick any doors!" she said hastily into her earpiece. "He's set a claymore behind at least one door."

"Understood," Harris replied.

It meant that they had to move almost painfully slowly as they swept the main floor. There were stairs leading down to a basement at the far end of the corridor, and Maya found herself flashing back to the basement of the apartment building. There were no lights there now, but she had her torch at least.

She and the other agents made their way downstairs, with Maya hoping that they might find *something*. Even now, there was a chance that the kidnapper might be huddled somewhere away from the teargas, with his captives.

What she found instead was a scene so familiar that it made her heart wrench to see it. A single chair sat in the middle of an otherwise empty box of a room, exactly the same way that it had in the apartment building in Pittsburg. On it, there was a single rectangle of cardboard, along with what appeared to be a piece of cloth. Keeping her eyes peeled for more traps, Maya made her way to that chair.

She stood there for a moment, debating with herself. By rights, she should leave all this to be picked up by a forensic team, yet she knew that they weren't the point of all this. It wouldn't be *them* the postcard was addressed to, and it certainly wasn't their sister who found herself in the hands of some madman. Making her decision, Maya reached out for the objects sitting on the chair.

She picked up the cloth first. Since the teargas seemed to have dissipated, she risked removing her gas mask. Instantly, she smelled the general floral scent of the place, but the cloth in front of her had an even stronger scent of violets. Strong enough that if it had been held next to someone who was blindfolded, it might be all they remembered of where they were taken to.

Maya barely even needed to glance at the postcard to recognize the familiar bunny motif. This time, they were hopping through a field of violets, in an obvious taunt. She had thought that small hint might be so significant. Reyes had thought he was so smart, tracking down the obvious place Liza could have smelled what she smelled. Yet here the kidnapper was, making it painfully obvious that she had scented only what he wanted her to. He'd laid a false trail and then probably watched them all run after it

On the back were just a few words, in the kidnapper's writing this time.

Which one will pay for your mistakes?

*

The man people called Frank sat in the control room of his bunker, watching dear Maya and her fellow agents on his screens for a few moments longer before he cut the signal. He could feel himself getting angry, his otherwise unremarkably handsome features twisting slightly with it.

He'd told them what to do and what not to do. They'd disobeyed him. Again.

He'd anticipated the first time, in Pittsburg. Some people needed to be shown that they were dealing with someone superior to them. That was normal. The second time, in the forest, when they had tried to trap him, had been more amusing than annoying, only demonstrating the incompetence of some of those Agent Grey worked with.

A third time, though? That was simply an insult. As if they didn't take him seriously.

He stood, leaving behind the bank of screens that stood at one side of a large, hemispherical room below his house. It was nowhere near the factory, although as soon as he'd seen that place, Frank had known that it might prove to be a useful decoy at some point.

He wasn't worried about the FBI tracking the camera signal. He'd made sure he used security cameras that were already installed, routed through a server employed by an actual security company so that it looked like a natural feed.

Making everything look natural was a skill Frank had learned early in life.

For now, he walked over to a circular space within the room, with a drain set at the center and a hook overhead. In his memories, Liza Carty still hung there, begging to be let down, begging for her life.

Those memories were almost enough to assuage the anger that Frank felt, but not quite. Nothing ever quite made that anger, that need for violence, go away, and now the FBI had roused it.

Maya had roused it.

Walking over to a table, he fetched his mask and his gloves, pulling them carefully into place, covering up every trace of himself. He took a stun gun with him, to stop any hint of rebellion from his bunnies. Even angry, Frank believed in being careful.

Not that he needed to be, when the FBI were so foolish.

Had they thought that he was an idiot? That he wouldn't realize that they would question any of his bunnies who were released? That dear Maya wouldn't question her frantically, trying to find any clue to the whereabouts of her sister? He'd given her something to remember, and then waited.

They'd broken the rules. A part of him had wanted to trigger some of the explosives in the place remotely, just to make that clear, but it had been hard to do so without risking injuring Agent Grey, and Frank still had uses for her.

No, the FBI would have to learn its lesson another way.

He unlocked the door to his control room, heading out into the tunnels of his underground bunker, lit by strip lights and smelling dead and dusty. He saw a flicker of movement as one of his bunnies tried to move out of his line of sight. Had she somehow picked up on his anger, or was she just cowering from him on general principles?

Frank didn't care. Instead, he went through to one of the main living spaces, bare except for a few sticks of furniture. None of his bunnies were there. Probably all of them wanted to avoid the risk of his anger. Perhaps they had seen that Liza Carty had disappeared from their little world and assumed that he had killed her. Perhaps they thought they would be next.

He took a hard backed chair and sat upon it.

"Come here!" he called out, in a deliberately sing-song voice. "Come here, my bunnies! I want to talk to you!"

They came, hesitantly and shuffling, each of the eleven remaining women clearly waiting for the others. None of them tried to stay away or hide, though. They knew the price of disobedience too well for that. They all wore identical jumpsuits, all had hair that was starting to tangle from their time underground. They were mostly thinner than they had been, even though Frank remembered to give them food... well, most days.

The eleven of them gathered around him, and Frank gestured to the floor around him like a teacher at story time. Well, he had a story to tell, after all. They only hesitated for a moment, but it was enough.

"Sit down!" he bellowed at them, and they did it, cowering back from the anger in him even if they couldn't see his face.

"My bunnies, my bunnies, what are we going to do with you?" Frank asked, looking around them carefully, observing the ways in which they cowered back. "I have bad news, my bunnies. The FBI tried to find us."

Which of them looked hopeful? Which of them looked afraid?

"I warned them not to, but they did it anyway. They broke the rules I gave them. And as you all know, when rules get broken, there has to be a punishment."

Now they *all* looked afraid, but Frank had already made his selection. He went over to one of them, catching her by the wrist and pulling her up.

"No, no, please!"

"Don't blame me, my dear. The FBI are the ones who did what they shouldn't, and now... well, now I'm going to have to send them a message."

CHAPTER FIVE

Maya avoided the debrief, because she was afraid of what she might say to Harris or Reyes in the wake of the raid. Instead, she went home, hit the small gym she'd set up in her apartment, and tried to use the burn of exercise to distract herself.

It didn't do a lot of good. Every time she hit the punchbag there, Maya found herself imagining that it was Reyes's face. Or Harris's. She'd told them both that this was a mistake, a trick, and they hadn't believed her.

Thud, thud, went her fists against the bag in a one-two.

That fear was simple: what would the kidnapper do?

Maybe nothing. Maybe he was bluffing. He'd issued a warning after the last raid, not hurt any of his captives. Then again, it was hard not to believe that a man was capable of violence when he left potentially lethal traps for people to walk into, and lured them in with fake evidence.

Maya's fists hammered the bag again, hard enough that it ached even through her bag gloves and wraps.

Briefly, Maya considered that evidence. They would test the piece of cloth he'd left, just as they did the postcards, but she was willing to bet that there wouldn't be much to find. She was more interested in the kind of mind that could do something like that, planting the memory of violets in Liza Carty's head so that she would remember it about the place where she'd been held, all to draw them to the factory and tell them again that they'd failed.

Maya circled the bag, treating it like an opponent, weaving and bobbing.

Did the kidnapper enjoy that part of it? Maya guessed that he had to, or why do it? Why not just leave no trace at all? It worried her that this was a man who set rules for them to follow, but then encouraged the FBI to break them by giving them clues. That said to Maya that he was a man looking to play sadistic games with them that they couldn't win, who liked to think of himself as orderly and neat, but who couldn't be relied upon to be fair with his own rules. This was someone who might be unpredictable and dangerous in the extreme.

She threw in a kick, hitting the bag hard with her shin, turning her hip over into it.

And he had her sister. The fear of what might happen to Megan was the worst part of it. Her only hope now was that the kidnapper somehow didn't know about the raid. They'd not put anything out over the usual frequencies for a scanner to pick up, so maybe that would be enough.

Even as Maya thought it, she knew that it wasn't likely. This was a man who seemed to know every detail of her life and investigations. Probably there was already a postcard waiting in her mailbox downstairs.

That thought made Maya slam another combination into the bag, imagining everything she would do if she ever got her hands on the man who had taken her sister, trying to tell herself not to give in to the anxiety this bastard so obviously wanted from her. Yet now that the thought was in her head, she couldn't leave it alone. She had to know. She had to check.

Maya headed downstairs to collect her mail, and every step felt as though it added to her anxiety. She reached her mailbox and froze, because there was something sitting inside it.

A large brown envelope sat in the mail box, with her name printed neatly on the front. There didn't seem to be a postcard anywhere in the box, so Maya dared to relax a little. She took the envelope upstairs with her, went into her apartment and got coffee while she opened it. It would probably be something from-

A postcard tumbled out, along with a collection of old-fashioned polaroid pictures that scattered over Maya's kitchen counter. Something else fell with them, clattering down among them and flashing gold against the light. It was a small locket in the shape of a rabbit, on a golden chain.

Maya froze in place at the sight of it, because there was only one person something like that could be from. She barely dared to touch it, partly because this might finally be a piece of evidence leading back to the kidnapper, partly because she didn't want this to be real. As much as she'd gone downstairs in the expectation of a postcard, Maya's *hope* had been that there would be nothing.

Now there was a postcard, and more. Maya's hands went to the postcard first, and just the image on the front told her that all her hopes that the kidnapper might not know about the raid were for nothing. He'd still drawn in a bunny, but now it was hopping around an image of the factory that she and the others had raided that morning. He was taunting her with the fact that he knew, as clearly as if he'd said it.

Barely daring to do it, Maya turned the postcard over, and saw the kidnapper's now familiar handwriting.

You made me do this when you tried to find me.

Made him do what? The thought of all the possibilities made a fresh wave of fear go through Maya. Was a woman dead? Was her *sister* dead? Was it more than one, with each of those photographs showing a murdered woman? Just the thought of the possibilities meant that Maya couldn't bring herself to look at the photographs right then.

To buy herself a few more moments before she had to do it, she fetched evidence gloves and opened the locket instead. It was empty inside save for a curling lock of blonde hair, kept there the way someone from way back might have kept the hair of a lover. Or the way a serial killer might have kept a trophy from a victim.

Working cold cases, it was impossible to ignore that side of things. Maya had seen enough killers who had taken things from their victims so that just the sight of the hair made her certain that a woman would be dead. Dead because of her, because she hadn't managed to think of a way to stop Harris from going ahead with the raid.

Eventually, though, she had to look at the photographs.

They showed a woman, pictured up close. Pictures so close, in fact, that it was impossible to make out who she was. Each photograph was like a crime scene image, carefully focusing on one particular piece of her flesh.

Each image showed an injury. There was a black eye, a split lip. There were bruises. There were welts that might have been from being struck with some kind of object. Each injury was catalogued as neatly and dispassionately as if this were some kind of art project, and not the savage beating of one of the women this monster had kidnapped. No, not savage, precise. Looking at the blows, Maya guessed that each one had been calculated, drawn out, delivered to make the message clear without ever quite risking killing the woman subjected to all of this.

Maya felt physically sick that this had happened to someone because of her. She had to fight to keep from running to the bathroom

25

and throwing up. This... this wasn't someone just playing sick games. This was a man who was proving exactly how easy he found it to hurt people in cold blood.

It was him giving a last warning, before he killed one of the women he'd captured.

Maya knew what she needed to do then. Not even bothering to change out of her workout clothes, she gathered up the things the kidnapper had sent, stuffed them back into the envelope, and set off for the FBI office.

*

Maya's fear and her anger fueled her as she headed upstairs to the fourth floor, then walked straight to Harris's office. He was in the middle of a call but Maya walked straight in anyway.

"-understand that, sir, but the budgetary considerations sometimes have to take a backseat to operational necessity." He waved Maya back, like his talk about the budget could ever count for more than this.

Maya opened the envelope and spread the photographs out in front of him. She saw Harris' eyes widen, his mouth hanging open at the sight of it all.

"Can I call you back, sir?" Harris said. "We have a situation here. Yes, thank you."

Maya watched while he stared at the photographs.

"What is all this?" Harris asked.

"This is what happened because we raided the factory," Maya said. "Another anonymous drop off in my mail."

She saw Harris pale at the sight of it, and that made Maya feel a little better about her boss. At least he understood the impact of the decision he'd made.

"Is there any away to ID the woman?" Harris asked. Of course he wasn't going to admit that he was wrong, and Maya knew better than to try to tell him. This was the most she was going to get.

Maya pointed to the locket. "There's a lock of hair in there. I'm assuming it's hers. We should be able to pull DNA."

Harris nodded. "All right. This is him showing us that we have to play by his rules, so we will, for now. Take all that down to forensics. See what they can get from it."

"And after that?" Maya asked.

Harris didn't look happy. "After that, I guess we have to wait for him to get in contact again."

*

Two days. Two days with no contact. It was enough to drive Maya mad with worry about her sister. Did the lack of contact mean that the kidnapper had changed his mind about all this? Had he decided that the time had come to cut his losses? Would the eleven women he still held simply disappear?

Those thoughts were enough that it was hard for Maya to focus on anything else. She had other work, because there were *always* cold cases out there waiting for her attention, but she couldn't concentrate for long enough on any of them to make headway. That was particularly frustrating because, ordinarily, Maya would have been driven, striving to try to make a difference by bringing in people who thought they'd gotten away with their crimes.

Whenever she got home, she checked her mail, usually more than once. Every takeout menu, bill, and piece of junk mail turned into a disappointment, with the first glimpse of it raising her hopes, and then the realization that it wasn't a postcard dashing them.

What was he waiting for? If this guy had taken twelve women, then presumably he wanted Maya to do more than one thing for him? If he had so many cold cases sitting in the wings, waiting for her to work on them, why not just *send* her the next one?

Maybe he just felt as though he had all the time in the world. Maybe he was that confident about how secure he was in his scheme. Maybe he assumed that no one would come close to catching him, and he was taking his time.

Or maybe he just enjoyed torturing Maya by making her wait, wondering what was happening to Megan in the meantime.

She tried to force herself to work, to do anything other than focus on the kidnappings. She went out grocery shopping, walking around the store and trying to pretend at least for now that things were normal.

It might have felt more normal if she hadn't immediately checked her mailbox when she got home. Again, there was that surge of excitement as she saw mail inside, followed by the sharp disappointment that came when there was no postcard there. She headed upstairs, letting herself into her apartment and setting down her bags of groceries in the kitchen.

Maya turned back towards the door and saw it, a shape catching at the corner of her eye. She looked again and saw it lying there, where it had obviously been pushed under her door. That made her look around sharply, checking that she was alone in the apartment. Somehow, a postcard pushed under the door seemed far more intrusive than one simply appearing in her mailbox.

The bunny motif was visible from where she stood, and Maya went over to it, lifting it up and holding it, barely daring to turn it over.

Finally the postcard she'd been waiting for was here. It seemed she had another case.

CHAPTER SIX

Maya took the postcard in to the FBI headquarters, moving with a purpose that she hadn't had for the last couple of days. She strode in, ready to work, ready to find out what the kidnapper had in store for her.

Harris must have seen the change in her as she walked in, because the deputy director came out to her, looking intrigued.

"What happened?" he asked.

Maya held up the postcard for him to see.

"Another warning, or…"

"He has a case for me," Maya said. She turned the postcard to show that it contained a name and address, written out in the same neat hand as usual. Samantha Neele, of Pollock, Louisiana. There was a date, too, less than a week away.

"Another deadline," Harris said, not sounding happy about it.

"We've already seen that he's serious, sir," Maya reminded him. "I don't think I can afford to be late on this one like last time."

She didn't add that it was especially true after the debacle of the raid. She needed to keep her boss on her side for this.

"I know we have to go along with this," Harris said. "I just don't like it. Giving in to this guy isn't getting us anywhere, not when the last victim he released died anyway."

Maya could understand that frustration, because she felt it too. She felt the fear that she might not get her sister back, even if she did everything the kidnapper wanted her to do.

"Is there any news on Liza Carty?" Maya asked.

"They're saying that the stress of everything she'd been through was just too much for her heart."

Which meant that he'd been reading the reports. Probably some of that was just that he'd been heading up the rescue mission, and wanted to know more. Maya suspected that some of it was that he felt a little guilty, too, for not doing more. Maya certainly did. If she'd found an answer sooner, would that have made it easier on Liza Carty?

No, she couldn't think like that. She had to focus on this new case. This was her chance to do things better.

29

"I should look up Samantha Neele," she said.

Harris went with her to her computer station, where Maya tapped in the name and the location. What she found caught her by surprise.

"Samantha Neele, killed eighteen months ago," she read out to Harris. "A corrections officer living in Pollock, Louisiana, and working at the federal prison nearby. Stabbed to death in her home."

"And they never found the killer?" Harris said.

That would have been normal, but in this case, Maya could only shake her head.

"That's the thing, sir. The local cops caught a guy for it, her boyfriend, and he's currently serving time for the murder. This isn't a cold case."

Ordinarily the only reason to open up something like this would be if some compelling new evidence came to light, if an appeal succeeded and opened the whole issue up again. Even Maya usually reasoned that if there was a bad guy in jail for a crime, her time was better spent chasing after the ones who hadn't been caught yet.

"But our kidnapper thinks that it is," Harris said, looking thoughtful. "He's saying... what? That the wrong guy has been convicted?"

"I assume so. But what does he know that we don't?"

Maybe plenty, given that he'd been a step ahead of them on everything else so far. Obviously *something* had convinced him that the wrong person had been convicted of this, but what?

And if he was right, did that mean that the wrong person had been sitting in jail for a year and a half? Was that a chance to save someone else in all of this?

"Do I investigate?" Maya said. "I have to, don't I, with everything that's at stake?"

Harris didn't look happy about it, but she saw him nod.

"Yes, I think you'll have to. We don't have any other choice. But if this is a closed case, we need to think of an angle that's going to let you look into it without problems of jurisdiction."

That was the other part of this: Maya couldn't just jump in and claim jurisdiction over any case she wanted. A murder like this, without any crossing of state lines, was a purely local matter.

And yet, there seemed to be an FBI file attached to the case.

Opening it, Maya looked through, and saw the reason at once: because Samantha Neele had been working as a corrections officer in a federal, not state, prison, it had been the death of a federal employee, and just enough to see the FBI called in. There was a brief note about a specialist unit from the bureau taking a look at the case, although no actual details of anything they'd found.

"This file looks as though it was just abandoned," Maya said. "The locals closed the case, but there's no sign of this file being closed."

"Politics," Harris said. His eyes glittered as he said it. "In this case, potentially *useful* politics."

"Sir?"

Harris understood this side of things far better than Maya did. Far better than she wanted to. She was in the job to try to find answers that had been left hidden for too long. She understood that side of it, and she enjoyed the action that came with the job too. The politics of making herself and the department look good mostly passed her by.

"If we didn't close the case, that's as good as saying that we didn't fully agree with the local investigation," Harris said. "But at the same time, something happened to make it less interesting to us."

"What could that be?" Maya asked.

She saw Harris shrug. "It could be a number of things, but most likely lack of resources. It's hard to justify keeping agents on a case when there's an answer out there already, even if the agents have doubts."

Like when Harris had tried to call her back to DC the moment they'd found Anne Postmartin's scumbag boyfriend.

"Some other case might have come up," Harris said. "Or maybe whatever caught their interest in the first place proved not to be there. My guess is that it might have been left open to allow them to come back to it if it turned out to link to some larger investigation after all."

"But *what* investigation?" Maya asked. The file was more sparse than it should have been, even with only a limited investigation.

"Hard to say," Harris said. "I'll try to find out. Probably the file is empty because the locals found an answer so quickly. Looking at it, by the time we got on the ground, the whole thing was wrapped up already."

"Does that mean that as soon as *I* get on the ground, they'll be pushing to get me out of there?" Maya asked.

"You know as well as anyone that local law enforcement usually cooperates with the FBI. Look at Detective… what was it? Spinoza?"

31

"Spinelli," Maya said. Marco had been cooperative, and friendly. Maybe even more than that. It was hard to stop thinking about him once she'd started.

"Him," Harris said. "Local PDs want the truth of these things as much as you do, Grey."

Maya wasn't so sure about that. Marco had been helpful back in Cleveland, but his department had only helped under duress. Worse, that had been in a case that was still unsolved. *This* was one where they thought they'd already found the killer.

"Relax, Grey," Harris said. "I'll call them while you're on your way, and explain the situation. I'm sure, once they understand what's at stake with all this, they'll be eager to cooperate."

Maya hoped so. With less than a week to solve this case, she could use all the help she could get.

*

Maya used the flight to Louisiana to review the case files on her laptop. The more she looked at them, the more of an affinity she felt for Samantha Neele.

This was a woman who had been a prison guard for several years, rising to a senior position through her efforts. Before that, it seemed that she'd seen action in the army. Those similarities made Maya feel as though she knew Samantha, even before she kept looking into what had happened.

The rest of the file seemed to set out a straightforward case against one Jonathan Dennis, known to everyone as J.D. After a three year relationship, Samantha had broken up with him. In a rage, he'd come home and stabbed her, with a single wound to the throat that had killed her quickly. He'd been an obvious suspect, with no alibi and a clear motive, found standing over the body after he'd called the cops in, and the local police hadn't wasted a moment in arresting him.

Maya could understand that, up to a point. Most murders weren't complex. The suspects, the motivations, the opportunities were usually all clear. She only saw the ones that went unsolved, but for every one that made it to be a cold case, there were dozens more that were solved quickly by local police or the FBI. Yet there didn't seem to be a huge amount of corroborating evidence that couldn't be explained another

32

way. Yes, Johnathan Dennis had his girlfriend's blood on him, but that might mean he'd tried to help her, not that he'd murdered her.

The whole thing raised red flags for Maya.

Maya took a moment to look out of the plane's windows, because looking meant that she could steel herself before turning to the crime scene photographs. The landscape below was mostly wetland and forest, far more vast and open than around Washington. Even from up here, it was hard to spot an end to the wilderness of it all.

Now Maya was ready to look, and as she looked, she was grateful that she'd taken a moment to prepare herself. She'd seen plenty of awful things before, but that didn't make the sight of death any better for her.

She saw Samantha lying there in her kitchen, dressed in jeans and a sweatshirt, covered in blood. It was the first image Maya had seen of her. She looked athletic and muscular, tough and able to fight. Yet someone had killed her, with a single knife blow to her throat.

The wound was awful to look at. The worst part of any wound for Maya was the wrongness of it, the gap where there should have been flesh. This was all of that and more, because of the pool of blood forming around Samantha's body, the look of horror in her still open eyes.

Maya had to force herself to look past all of that, trying to take in the rest of the crime scene. There were yellow evidence tags everywhere. The kitchen was utterly disturbed in a way that suggested a fight had taken place there, with plates broken on the floor, cups and glasses scattered across the floor.

Samantha Neele had seen her killer coming, and had tried to fight. That, or an argument had built up slowly, and then the final blow had come out of nowhere. Actually, looking at the photographs of the body, that explanation made more sense to Maya, because she couldn't see signs of the defensive wounds on her arms that would have come if Samantha had been trying to protect herself.

Maya tried to imagine what it would have been like for her. As a corrections officer, she would have been tough, used to being able to protect herself. Yet she'd been killed by a single strike that came out of nowhere.

There was a kind of fear that came with that for Maya, because it was all too easy to imagine it happening to herself. She was tough, had taken down plenty of bad guys with her hands, or her sidearm. She could fight, but just this one photograph showed how easily that could turn out not to be enough.

Maya had to remind herself that this wasn't about her. Looking out of the window again, she could see the plane closing on its destination rapidly, the city of Alexandria there in the distance, with the forests that contained Pollock to the north of it. It was about getting there, and finding answers. It was about Samantha Neele, about whoever had killed her, and about the woman whose life hung in the balance if she didn't solve this.

CHAPTER SEVEN

Maya landed in Alexandria, Louisiana, and this time, there wasn't a good looking local cop waiting to welcome her. There wasn't *any* kind of welcome, other than the humid heat of the place, which seemed strange to Maya. Harris had said that he would get in contact with the local police and, usually, that would mean that they would want to talk to her.

Maya wanted to talk to *them*. She only had a limited time in which to solve this case, and doing it would require all the help that she could get. The more that the local PD could tell her about the case, the better the chance there was of finding the real truth of it.

Assuming there was a real truth to find. The kidnapper seemed certain enough to send her there, but what if Jonathan Dennis had actually done this? Would that be enough to satisfy the man who held her sister?

Maya found herself wishing that Marco Spinelli were there with his beat-up Explorer, there to give her a ride and help her with the case. She shook off that thought, though, and went to hire a car. That got her a maroon Toyota, in which she cranked the AC high and drove north, up through Ball and towards Pollock, along roads that cut through the surrounding forest, with turnings promising to take her to one of the lakes that seemed to be the main attractions in the areas.

It didn't take long to get there, past a road that held signs for both the prison and an airbase. It was a tiny place, barely more than a few streets, with most of its stores given over to fishing or camping supplies, designed to let people out into the landscape beyond. It had a run-down look to it, like it hadn't been pulling in the tourist trade that it wanted. Maya guessed that most of the people there went into one of the nearby cities to work, maybe over as far as Shreveport. She spotted a couple of general stores, a diner, and not much else.

This was where Samantha Neele had lived, presumably because it had been convenient for the prison at which she worked. Maya tried to imagine living somewhere as small as this, and she couldn't manage it.

35

She'd spent so long living in big cities that it was hard to imagine living anywhere without the ease and convenience that went with them.

She drove past the address where Samantha had lived, one of a row of wooden built houses, raised up to avoid any problems of flooding from the local wetlands. They were all simply built, most with old trucks or beaten-up cars parked outside rather than anything more expensive. That didn't surprise Maya, because it didn't seem to her like the kind of place people stayed if they made a lot of money.

From a police standpoint, small had its advantages. It reduced the number of people who could be potential suspects. It meant that there was more chance of a neighbor noticing if someone strange came into town. It had downsides too, of course: Maya wasn't going to be able to trawl through the array of CCTV footage that she might have had in the middle of a big city, and there was always a risk in such close knit communities that people wouldn't want to talk to her.

Still, she'd have the local police department to help with that.

As she drove over there, it occurred to Maya that she was a lot less hostile to the idea of local help this time around than she had been back in Cleveland. Maybe it was just that she'd seen how much it was possible for someone who already knew a case to help, or maybe it was just those fond memories of Marco intruding on her usual skepticism.

Either way, Maya felt fairly optimistic as she pulled up outside the local police department. Ok, so it was small, not really much bigger than one of the general stores; and ok, it was a little run down around the edges, with peeling paint on the sign saying "Sherriff's Department," but what did she expect, in somewhere so small? Once she got in there, she was sure she would find *someone* who wanted the truth on this found as badly as she did.

She walked in and found a wood paneled main room, with an old reception counter, which a couple of cops were waiting near, along with a straggly bearded, skinny perp in handcuffs. The man behind the desk was an older cop who looked pretty out of shape. Probably he didn't get out from behind there much.

"Zeke, how many times do the guys have to bring you in for stealing from other guys' traps?"

"It wasn't me!"

"Sure it wasn't. Cell three, boys." The cop looked over in Maya's direction. "What can I do for you, ma'am? Got lost on your way to the air strip or the penitentiary?"

36

Maya took out her ID, and watched the cop's expression shift pretty much immediately, hardening into something far less friendly.

"What's the FBI doing here?" he asked.

"I'm here to speak to the sheriff," Maya explained. "Agent Grey, FBI cold case unit."

The cop gave a shrug, as if she wasn't even worth the words anymore, then pointed through to the interior of the station. Maya set off towards it.

"Sheriff Recks won't be happy to see you," the cop warned her, as if that would get Maya to turn around and leave.

Instead, she headed into the main office of the place, not quite big enough to call a bullpen, not much more than a couple of desks and trio of doorways leading off deeper into the station.

The man who sat behind one of the desks wearing a sheriff's uniform was probably in his late forties, with steel gray hair cut military short, piercing blue eyes and the heavy build of someone who worked out a lot, but ate too much to make up for it. He stood as Maya approached, starting with a smile that faded quickly as Maya took out her ID.

"*You're* the FBI agent?" he asked, in a tone that made it clear he didn't believe it. Or maybe he just didn't think the FBI should have hired anyone like her.

"Agent Maya Grey. And you're Sheriff Recks?"

He nodded, but didn't venture anything more.

"My boss should have called you," Maya said. "To let you know what's happening?"

She hoped that Harris had managed to do it. With the FBI, there was always the chance that some kind of emergency might have gotten in the way. Still, with everything that was at stake, Maya wanted to believe that her boss would have made every effort he could to get through.

"He told me," Sheriff Recks said. "Only one problem for your little cold case unit, Agent: this isn't a cold case. We caught the guy who did this."

"We have reason to believe that there might be more to this," Maya said.

She heard the sheriff snort derisively.

"What reason? What could you possibly have that means we should just ignore the trial and conviction of Jonathan Dennis? I worked that case, Agent, so it had better be good."

Maya wondered how much to tell the sheriff. It didn't sound as though Deputy Director Harris had decided to share the details of the kidnappings. Maybe once he'd met the initial hostility, he'd decided not to give the sheriff anything that would get them shut out of this.

"The murder has come up in connection with another case, and a reliable source has told us that Jonathan Dennis might not be the real killer." A reliable source? Was that really what Maya thought the kidnapper was? Not reliable, but he seemed to know more than anyone else about these cases. He seemed to know enough to be sure that this was something she had to look at.

"Then your source isn't very reliable," Sheriff Recks said. "Because J.D. was dead to rights. His girlfriend killed, after they'd argued, in a house where he was found standing over her body. Open and shut. In this case *shut*."

Maya guessed what it would be like for a small town sheriff. He'd probably never worked a murder before or since. He was probably desperately attached to the one he *had* solved, but Maya couldn't just ignore this when lives were at stake.

"I still have to look into it," Maya said.

The sheriff stood then. He was a big man, only a little taller than her since she wasn't exactly short, but broad with it.

"Now listen here, missy."

Missy? Was *that* his problem with her?

"Agent," Maya replied.

"You can call yourself what you like," Sheriff Recks said, his voice rising slightly. "But I'm still the sheriff here. This is *my* jurisdiction, and it was *my* case. A case that is now closed, because the bastard who did this is in jail."

It was hard for Maya not to rise to the provocation and raise her voice in turn.

"There is an open FBI file on the case," she said. "One that did not close with the conviction. Given the connection to another case, that means that I have every right to investigate here. I'd prefer your cooperation with that, Sheriff."

"Oh, I'm sure you would," Sheriff Recks said. "But you aren't going to get it, unless it's with a ride back to the airport so that you can go back to DC and leave things well enough alone."

Well enough alone. Those were three words Maya had heard plenty of times from people when she was working cold cases. Even a few times from cops. Right now, though, they weren't even going to be close to enough to stop her from doing her job.

"What are you so threatened by, Sheriff?" she asked. "Afraid I'll make you look bad if I find out that you arrested the wrong guy?"

She could see that hit a nerve.

"We arrested the *right* guy," the sheriff said. "J.D. even admitted that he was there in the house that night. He was *there*, agent. He had the means, the opportunity, the motive."

"Did he confess?" Maya asked. "If he was so quick to admit that he was there, did he also admit that he did it?"

"Of course not," Sheriff Recks replied, in a tone that made it clear he didn't think much of the question. "Do your suspects all confess to what they've done, Agent? Is that how things work up in the big city?"

So that was another part of it. He didn't like that some big city agent had come in to try to interfere in the little corner of the world he controlled.

"You'd be surprised," Maya said, thinking about her last case. She thought a moment longer. "He *never* confessed? Not even when it was obvious that he was going to go down for the murder? Not when it might have gotten him a deal for less time?"

"We don't do deals with killers here, Agent." The sheriff looked offended at the very prospect of it. "We give them what they deserve. *This* one got what he deserved."

"Then what physical evidence did you have?"

"He was standing over her body, covered in her blood."

"You mean the same way someone might have been if they'd tried to save the victim's life?" Maya pointed out.

"Trust me, you don't know J.D. That isn't what he was doing."

Maya realized that she wasn't going to get any help here.

"Thank you for your time, Sheriff," she said. "If you let me have access to your files, I'll let you know how I get on with my investigation."

He took a step between her and the door. "Let's be clear about this. The position of sheriff around here is elected, and I'm up for re-election this year. That means I'm *not* going to let someone just walk in and start trying to make me look bad by ripping apart one of my cases. Understood?"

Maya looked him in the eye. "I understand you very well, Sheriff. But I'll still want to see your files."

For several seconds, she thought that he might refuse, might even try to throw her out of his station, but he didn't. Instead, he turned to his desk and grabbed a slender file.

"I got this out when your boss called. Read it, and *then* tell me I'm wrong. Or better yet, read it and then get out of my town."

Maya took the file and walked past him, ignoring the angry look he gave her. Whatever the sheriff said, the kidnapper was sure that there was something in this, and right now, like it or not, *his* was the opinion that mattered. He was the one whose whim would determine whether her sister lived or died.

That meant that she had to solve this, regardless of what the local cops thought.

CHAPTER EIGHT

Maya strode from the police station, determined to try to make some sense of everything that was going on here. She wasn't going to let the hostility of a few local cops stop her.

Better, she had the case file. How much more did she *need* from the local PD beyond that? If she needed forensics here, they would have to be sent off to Shreveport or Baton Rouge in any case. She could send them to a local FBI office just as easily. Ok, so it would have been easier to have some local knowledge on her side, but there were upsides to that, too. At least she wasn't going to walk into whatever grudges any of the local people had against the police.

Because she couldn't use the sheriff's offices, Maya headed for the local diner, ordered the shrimp and some coffee, then set down the file in front of her, determined to find anything there that hadn't made it into the versions she'd read on the computer. The diner was run down and pretty much empty except for a bored looking waitress and an old guy doing a crossword in one corner.

Maya focused on the file. There wasn't much to read, because the file was so sparse; it barely counted as one. Even so, Maya went over the details carefully. She found a transcript of the original 911 call, made by Jonathan Dennis the morning after the murder.

My girlfriend. I've just come back and I've found her... oh God. You've got to send someone.

A note in what Maya assumed was the sheriff's handwriting sat beside it reading simply:

Trying to cover it up. Sat there all night, thinking of what to say.

Was that what he'd been doing, or was that genuinely the kind of shock that happened when someone came back to find someone they loved had been murdered? Maya didn't know, wasn't going to even *pretend* to be able to tell from a transcript, but it did seem to her that the sheriff had dismissed Jonathan Dennis's panicked call pretty quickly.

Which begged the question of what made Sheriff Recks so certain that it was him. Maya turned to the sheriff's report next:

41

I responded to the call at 8:45am. Arriving at the property, I saw that the perimeter was secure, so I entered the house with Deputy Stevens. I found Jonathan Dennis standing over the body of Samantha Neele, with dried blood on his hands. Questioning him, he admitted that he had been in the house the night before. When we asked Ms. Neele's family about her, we found evidence that her relationship with Mr. Dennis was argumentative, and that they had broken up.

That was what he had on Jonathan Dennis? Just that he was there? Wanting to make sure, Maya kept looking through the file. She checked the file's copy of the coroner's report, but it just matched the one that she had already seen.

She checked the forensics files on the killing next. The blood on Jonathan Dennis's hands had indeed matched Samantha Neele's. There was a section on the likely weapon used, most probably some kind of large hunting knife. There was a note in the file that no such weapon had been found on Dennis, or in the house. Maya saw another note from Sheriff Recks.

We conducted a search of the surrounding area, but were unable to locate the murder weapon. Our theory is that J.D. got rid of the weapon in the bayou when he decided to blame the murder on an outside killer.

He wrote 'got rid of the weapon in the bayou' in a way that made it sound obvious that it was impossible to find now that it had gone in there. Having flown over the expanse of it, Maya could imagine the difficulty of trying to find one knife among all of that. Even so, it bothered her that the weapon was missing.

Maya looked through the rest of it, trying to see why the sheriff had been so certain that he'd caught the right man. There was no clear connection of physical evidence that Maya could see.

What wasn't there was as telling to Maya as what was. There wasn't a long report on how many other avenues the sheriff had explored. There wasn't anything about another suspect in the main report. There didn't even seem to have been a concerted effort to find other reasons that Samantha Neele might have been killed.

Instead, it seemed that the sheriff had latched onto a theory early and not looked past it. The sheriff had told himself the story of a killer found standing over a corpse, rather than a boyfriend who had found his girlfriend killed and panicked. He had then sold that story to a judge and jury.

42

The trial report was quick and to the point, noting the successful conviction. Maya could imagine that trial all too easily, with the weakest public defender the state had been able to find, and probably a friendly judge. The sheriff had stood up and told them what he'd seen, while the prosecutor had set out the few pieces of forensic evidence.

After that, the result had come through quickly. Maybe a better lawyer might have been able to pick apart the prosecution's case, or maybe if the sheriff had kept going with his investigation, he might have found evidence pointing to someone else. It was clear that the sheriff had wanted *someone* to go down for this, and Jonathan Dennis had been such an obvious candidate that he hadn't looked for anyone else.

Maybe that was a good thing, though, because it meant that there were more avenues to explore.

"You can't have all that out in here," the waitress said. "You'll put off the other customers."

Maya looked around pointedly at the otherwise empty diner, but she still went to put the file away. As she was doing so, her eyes fell on a note towards the back, in Sheriff Recks' handwriting.

So much for the FBI's Moonlight Killer Theory.

Those words made Maya grab for the file, reading through, finding a whole extra page about FBI involvement that mostly seemed to be a complaint from the sheriff about them being there. She looked at the date of the murder, then used her phone to check it against the phases of the moon, waiting with bated breath for the answer. When it came through, she stared at the screen for a second or two, barely able to believe it.

Samantha Neele had been killed on the night of the full moon. The night when the Moonlight Killer made all his kills. The serial killer had slipped away from all detection so far, and no one knew quite how many people he'd killed.

The last case she'd been sent on had a possible connection to him too. Was the kidnapper trying to get her to catch the Moonlight Killer?

Maya tried to tell herself that it didn't necessarily mean anything. There was a reason the FBI investigation had left so quickly, after all. Even so, she picked up the file and hurried outside, calling her boss as she went.

Harris picked up quickly. "Grey, you're on the ground in Louisiana? How are things looking?"

43

"Mostly unfriendly," Maya said. "The local sheriff *really* doesn't like me being here."

"I got that impression when I called him," Harris said. "But I don't think he'll contest the jurisdiction. You also asked me what the specialist unit was that was assigned to this case."

"It was the one searching for the Moonlight Killer."

There was a pause on the other end of the line. "How did you know?"

"There's a note in the sheriff's copy of the case file," Maya explained, "and when I checked, Samantha Neele was killed on the night of the full moon. Does this mean that you're looking at the report from the team assigned to the case?"

"What there is of it," Harris said. "I think at this stage, they checked *every* killing that took place when there was a full moon, just in case it might lead them to the killer they were hunting."

Maya tried to imagine that level of commitment from the FBI team, hunting down any case that fit one broad criterion.

"That could be dozens of cases a year," Maya said. Any random murder on one or two days a month, from a drive by shooting to a careful poisoning.

"A lot of them didn't get past this initial look," Harris said. "Anything that seemed to be obviously someone else was ignored."

"But they left the case file open in case they were wrong." For which Maya was more than grateful. It meant that she had a chance to actually investigate this, when she suspected that Sheriff Recks just wanted to drive her to the county line and make sure that she never came back.

"So tell me what you make of the case," Harris said. "Do you think it could be the Moonlight Killer?"

Maya could hear the excitement in her boss's voice. He'd been just as excited the last time the Moonlight Killer had come up, in her previous case. He obviously relished the thought that one of his agents might be on the hunt for a killer who no one else had been able to catch, and who had already killed plenty of victims, even if the exact number was hard to pin down.

"It's too early to say, sir," Maya said, because she didn't want to wipe away the possibility just yet. Even so, she could see why the FBI team had rejected this case. It wasn't just that a plausible suspect had already been found, it was the whole method of the killing. The

Moonlight Killer's usual MO was strangulation, and if there was a deviation from that, what did it leave to tie this to him beyond the timing?

Was that enough?

Maya didn't know. She was more interested in the fact that, for the second case in a row, she found herself investigating murders where the FBI had considered the possibility that the Moonlight Killer was involved. That couldn't be a coincidence.

"How are you going to proceed, having seen things on the ground?" Harris asked.

"I can't rely on local help, so I'm going to have to take this on alone," Maya said.

"Going solo, Grey? I thought we talked about you needing a partner?"

They had, plenty of times.

"But I don't have one here," Maya argued, "so working this alone is what I have. I can handle it, sir."

"I'm not doubting that. It's just that if you need backup, you're a long way from DC."

"I don't think the local cops will just abandon me if I find myself in the middle of a firefight," Maya said, although truthfully, she wasn't entirely sure. The sheriff really hadn't wanted her here. "Sir, can you find out if Sheriff Recks knew the judge on this case well?"

"You're thinking about some kind of collusion?" Harris asked.

Maya hesitated before calling it that, because she was there to investigate a murder, not delve into the depths of the justice system here. "It just feels as though the whole case got an easier ride than it should have. I don't like the holes in the case against Jonathan Dennis."

"I'll check," Harris said. "Although even if I find that the sheriff and the judge knew one another, I'm not sure it proves anything."

Lack of proof seemed to be the problem all through this case. It seemed as though a conviction had been spun out of cobwebs and supposition. Maya wanted to know why.

"What will you be doing while I check?" Harris asked.

"I'll get started," Maya replied. "I want to get to know the victim. I want to find out if there was anyone else in her life who had a reason to kill her."

"And how are you going to do that?" Harris asked.

"I'm going to start by talking to her family."

45

CHAPTER NINE

As Maya pulled up in front of one of a row of identical wooden framed houses, she hoped that she would meet a better reception from Samantha Neele's parents than from the local cops.

If she was going to find her killer before the kidnapper's deadline, she would need *someone's* help.

To Maya it seemed almost strange that the address she had for Samantha Neele's family was just a couple of streets over from her own former residence, and not just because she suspected that a lot of people wouldn't have wanted to stay near the site of their daughter's murder. That was probably just because of the amount of time she'd spent away from her own family, though, first with the army, then living and working in DC.

The door was already opening as Maya approached the house, revealing a solidly built woman in her late fifties with dyed black hair, a worn expression, and a slight toughness to her features that reminded Maya of the pictures of Samantha. She was wearing an apron over a light colored dress, dusted with flour like she'd been baking.

"Hello," Maya said. "I'm Agent Maya Grey, with the FBI, and I wanted to talk to you about-"

"Sheriff Recks said I shouldn't bother talking to you," she said, before Maya could even get out the rest of it.

That caught Maya a little by surprise, and also made her bite back on her anger. She was used to unfriendly welcomes from local cops, but for one to actively try to stop her investigation before it started? The only thing that assuaged some of that anger was the other woman's body language. It wasn't pushing her away completely, didn't fit with her words.

"And do you plan on doing what Sheriff Recks says?" Maya asked. "I really need to talk to you, Ms. Neele. I want to know more about Samantha."

She had to wait while Samantha's mother made up her mind, and even though it was probably only a few seconds, it was still enough to make Maya worry. What if she wouldn't talk to her? How easy would it be to go through a whole investigation without *any* cooperation from the family, especially when the local police department didn't want to know either?

"All right," she said. "Come in, Agent Grey. Come through to the kitchen. I was just baking."

Maya went inside. The kitchen smelled of warm bread and spices, and even though it was pretty large, every surface was covered in mixing bowls and dough.

"That's a lot of baking," Maya said.

Samantha's mother shrugged. "It keeps me busy, and I earn a little selling it. Every little helps, since the divorce."

"When did that happen?" Maya asked.

"When do you think?" She took out a lump of dough and started kneading it. Maya didn't know if it actually required it or not, but she guessed the action was there for Ms. Neele to have something to take her frustrations out on.

Maya realized what must have happened. She'd seen it before, working cold cases. "The pressure of everything that happened drove you apart?"

"Of my daughter's *murder*," Ms. Neele said, pummeling the dough. "You can say it, although God knows Peterson couldn't. He couldn't stand being here either. Said we should both move away from Pollock and go somewhere else. Abandon the place we've lived all our lives. Abandon Samantha."

"You and your daughter were very close," Maya guessed. It didn't take much guessing. This was a woman who had chosen to keep living only a couple of streets over from her parents, and whose mother wanted to stay there to maintain the memory of her.

From the sound of it, her father had taken the opposite approach, coping with his grief by not wanting to be there.

"We were... we were more like best friends than mother and daughter, sometimes," Ms. Neele said. "Oh, I know everyone says that, but it was true. We would go out together on some of her days off, out to Alexandria sometimes. She told me everything about her life."

"Everything?" Maya said, and she found herself hoping it was true. The more Samantha's mother knew about what was going on in her daughter's life, the more of a chance there was that she might know something that would help find out the truth of all this.

48

"Everything," Ms. Neele said. "For a while, she used to hold back, used to say 'Mom, I work with bad people, you don't want to hear all about them.' But I did. It was a part of her, so I wanted to hear about it. She loved her job, you know."

"What did she love about it?" Maya asked. Being a corrections officer seemed like a tough job to do, even to her.

"She liked being able to make a difference, keeping people safe by keeping bad people locked up," Ms. Neele said. "But she also liked being able to make a difference in their lives. She used to say that most of them were going to be back in society at some point, so why not treat them like people, so they don't forget how to *be* people?"

That seemed a lot less jaded than some of the prison guards Maya had met in the past. It was a job that wore people down, yet it seemed that Samantha hadn't been burned out by it the way so many people were.

The more Maya heard about her, the more she felt a connection to the other woman.

"Even so, there must have been difficult parts to the job," Maya said.

"Some." Ms. Neele paused in her kneading. "She had to be tough too. It was a job she had to take seriously, because there are some very dangerous people over at the prison. One slip, and there were always people willing to try to hurt her."

That caught Maya's interest, but only for a moment. Samantha Neele had been killed in her own home. All her prisoners had just about the best alibi it was possible to have. It couldn't have been one of them.

"Was there anyone else who might have had a reason to hurt Samantha?" Maya asked. "Anyone who had a grudge against her? Did she have any enemies?"

Ms. Neele gave her a sharp look. "Agent Grey, I *know* who killed my daughter. J.D. has been tried and convicted for the crime. He's sitting in the same prison Samantha used to work at, rotting away for what he's done."

"You seem very certain it was him," Maya said. "As I understand it, he has never admitted the crime."

The other woman went back to her kneading. Maya got the feeling that hit a nerve. That was understandable. Maya digging into this risked undermining the closure that Samantha's mother had gotten when it came to her death.

"No, he hasn't even had the decency to do that. My daughter's dead, and he's just like so many others in there, protesting his innocence. I *know* he did it, though. Do you know why? Because she was sick of him being a deadbeat. She broke up with him, and he killed her for it. Then he pretended like he was just the one who found her body. Can you imagine what kind of sick mind it must take to do that?"

Unfortunately, Maya could. She'd gone through cases where that had happened back when she'd been training. People thought that if they pretended they'd just found the body, it explained away all the physical evidence and put them in the clear, even though it pointed the attention of the police straight at them. It was a high stakes game, and it was easy to imagine that Jonathan Dennis might have tried it, only for it to backfire.

The only problem was that, if that were the case, why would the kidnapper send Maya a postcard?

"If Samantha had broken up with J.D., what was he doing there that night?" Maya asked.

Ms. Neele shrugged. "Aside from killing my daughter? He sold her some nonsense about wanting to get back together with her. About having changed. All so that he could get close enough to kill her. Or maybe he actually meant that part. Maybe he went there, Samantha told him no, and he couldn't take it. That's what the sheriff thinks. You don't think there are men like that out there, Agent Grey?"

Maya knew that there were plenty, but this investigation was going to be hard if everyone was so convinced that it was J.D. that they wouldn't give Maya anything else. She needed to find a way to take this conversation in another direction.

"I know the local sheriff thought it was him," Maya said. "But I have to explore every other possibility. I have to do my job properly. I have to take it seriously."

She deliberately echoed the other woman's words.

"I know you do," Ms. Neele said, seeming to relent a little. "But what other possibilities? Why are you here, Agent Grey?"

"We've had… information come up," Maya said. "With a source suggesting that this case is not all it seems. I have to be here."

She hated having to put it like that, but there was no way she was going to explain all about the kidnapping.

"My Samantha was the same. When there was a job to be done, it didn't matter if she didn't like it, or if it was hard, she just got on with it. But I don't see who else you think it might have been."

Maya knew that if she didn't ask the next question then, she would probably never get to ask it.

"I know some people were talking about the Moonlight Killer. There's a note on the file about the possibility."

"People say all kinds of things," Ms. Neele said. "And folk around here have too much time on their hands. She was killed on the night of the full moon, so they all want to entertain themselves with rumors rather than looking at the real killer right in front of them. Even your FBI people left it alone quickly enough."

That was true. They'd looked briefly and then walked away as soon as they'd seen that a suspect was in custody. Maya wasn't about to.

"Are you sure there's no chance that there's a connection?" she asked. "Can you remember what some of the rumors were?"

This time, Ms. Neele picked up the dough and slammed it down on the worktop. "Agent Grey, do you think I want to believe rumors when, this way, I know who killed my daughter. That's what you're doing by coming here. You're taking that away."

Maya understood that part, at least. Normally, her work gave families closure, but this time, she was threatening to take that closure away by showing that the man currently in prison for killing Samantha Neele had spent a year and a half behind bars for nothing.

"If the Moonlight Killer killed my daughter," Ms. Neele said, "then suddenly, the man who did it isn't in prison. He's out there, and all the resources of the FBI haven't been able to catch him. No, it can't be him."

"I understand that," Maya said. "But I also think you're someone who values the truth. Is there anything else about the night your daughter died that you can tell me, Ms. Neele?"

"No, there's nothing."

There was a flicker of something in her face as she said it, though. A glance away, a slight tightening of her jaw muscles. It was nothing conclusive, but it didn't fit, and Maya knew that she couldn't let it go.

"What is it?" she asked. "You hesitated. What was it about that night?"

"It's…" Ms. Neele hesitated again.

51

"Please," Maya said. "I just want the truth of all this. If it turns out that J.D. really is the killer, then great, and if it turns out to be the Moonlight Killer, I'll hunt him down, whatever it takes."

Because her sister wouldn't survive otherwise.

"I believe you would," Ms. Neele said. "All right. Samantha called me that night. She called and said that she was going to get back together with J.D."

Which didn't fit with the idea that J.D. had killed her after she had refused to get back together with him. It was possible that she had changed her mind, but was it likely that she would call her mother, tell her that, and then go back on it?

Maya didn't know what all of it meant, but if she was going to find out the truth, she knew exactly where she needed to go next.

CHAPTER TEN

Arranging a visit to the prison was easier than Maya had expected. There was always a danger, with the need for security, that such a visit might take days to set up, and right now she didn't *have* days.

The active investigation made things more straightforward, though. It meant that she could drive straight over to USP Pollock, down the airbase road, and pull up in front of the huge gray expanse of the place.

It had multiple wings, and guard towers sticking up over what Maya assumed were exercise yards. Out front there was open greenery, but she noted that most of the trees nearby had been cleared away, presumably so that in the unlikely event of an escape, it would be harder for the inmates to just disappear from sight among the foliage. It was a solid, forbidding looking place; but then, Maya guessed that it was supposed to be.

Inside, the reception area was clean, open, and largely empty. There was a guard in a reception station, behind toughened glass. He was maybe forty, with tough features and a close shaved skull. Maya showed him her credentials.

"Agent Grey, FBI. I'm here to speak with one of your prisoners. Jonathan Dennis."

"Very well, ma'am," the guard said, and gestured to a door to Maya's left. "After we search you, a guard will come to lead you to a room where you can speak with the prisoner."

"Search me?" Maya said.

"We have to be very careful about contraband. You'll have to leave your service weapon behind. There are secure lockers."

"But I'm FBI," Maya insisted.

"And out there that matters," the guard said with an expression that suggested he didn't think it mattered much at all. "In here, what matters is controlling the environment, so the prisoners don't pose a threat. Hand over your weapon, or you don't get in."

Maya sighed. She hated the thought of being parted from her Glock, not least at the instruction of someone who seemed to be enjoying her discomfort. Worse, she was about to step into a place that was, by definition, filled with dangerous people. Yet she also couldn't spend all day here, arguing with the guard.

"All right," Maya said. She locked away her weapon in the locker the guard showed her to, allowed him to pat her down, then waited for him to hand her off to another guard so that she could get on with this.

That guard was a little younger, and a little friendlier.

"So, you're FBI?" he said. "I've always thought about trying for it. You must see a lot of action."

Maya shrugged. "I work cold cases. It's mostly talking to people."

She glossed over the part where a few days ago she'd been on an armed raid, and over the dangerous situations she'd been in over the days before that.

"Through here," the guard said, gesturing to an interview room.

There was a steel table bolted to the floor, and a couple of plastic chairs. It was empty other than that. Maya spotted the camera in one corner, watching for trouble.

"If you wait here, the prisoner will be here in a moment," the guard said. "I'll be outside when you're ready to leave."

Maya waited, rehearsing what she would ask Johnathan Dennis. She wanted to know about that night from his perspective. She wanted to hear the side of it that the sheriff's department wouldn't tell her.

They brought him in, wearing an orange prison jumpsuit, shackled and handcuffed. He was thirty four, the same age Samantha would have been now, but he looked older. There were lines on his face etched there by worry or lack of sleep, while he had dark rings under his eyes and a straggly beard that didn't suit him. Standing straight, he might have been as tall as Maya, but he seemed to stoop slightly as he walked.

The guard with him led him to a chair, sat him down, and cuffed him in place. Johnathan Dennis moved with a shuffling gait, letting it all happen. It was obvious to Maya from one look that prison life had not been kind to him.

"J.D.?" she said.

That seemed to catch his attention. "The guards don't call me that. I'm always just Dennis, or prisoner."

"But J.D. is what you prefer, right?" Maya said. She guessed that no one had asked him what he preferred about anything in the last eighteen months.

He nodded, but didn't answer.

54

"I'm Agent Grey, with the FBI cold cases unit," Maya said.

J.D. didn't even look at her.

"I was hoping that you could tell me what happened that night."

She didn't specify which night. After so long in here for the killing, there was only one night that mattered.

"What's the point?" he said, still not looking at her.

"I'd like to hear it," Maya said. "I'm looking into what happened, and I need to hear as many details as possible."

He shrugged. "Why? You won't believe me. I've told people a hundred times, and they don't believe me."

What must it have been like, not being believed for so long? Prison was full of people protesting their innocence, so it was only natural that people would treat J.D. like he was just one more guy spinning a story about how he didn't deserve to be there. Maybe he even was, but Maya wanted to be certain.

"I'd like you to tell me," Maya said. "I'm not the local sheriff's department. I'm a fresh set of eyes on this case, but to do my job, I need to hear about what happened. I can't help you if you don't help me."

"No one can help me," J.D. said.

"Maybe, but what exactly do you have to lose? Tell me what happened, J.D. Tell me all of it. I can't get to the truth if no one will tell me anything."

For a moment or two, Maya thought that he might not say anything, that prison had broken him too completely for him to put any trust in anyone. Then he straightened up a little, and actually managed to look her in the eye.

"Yeah, whatever. What do you want to know?"

"Walk me through it," Maya said. "Let's start with you and Samantha. You broke up, right?"

She saw him nod.

"Yeah. She didn't like the way I lived my life. I'd been in trouble a few times, kept hanging around with the same bunch of guys. She kept telling me I should change my life. I kept telling her there wasn't no way of changing nothing out here. Maybe if we moved somewhere, but there was always this place. And her parents."

That sounded like the kind of thing that could drive a relationship apart. Putting work first had certainly done enough to damage Maya's relationships over the years. But it also didn't feel like enough.

"What was the trigger?" Maya asked. "What actually made you break up?"

"She... uh... might have found out about a one night stand I had a couple of months before. Man, she ditched me pretty quick when she found out about that."

That seemed like a much more immediate reason to stop seeing someone. The kind of reason she could imagine Sheriff Recks understanding. No wonder he thought that J.D. was the killer.

"So Samantha broke up with you the day before her death?" Maya asked. She wanted to hear it from him, but more than that, she wanted to encourage him to remember any details that hadn't already been gone through a dozen times.

"Broke up with me, told me that she never wanted to see me again, the whole bit," J.D. said. Maya heard him sigh. "I don't even blame her."

He sounded as though he meant it. Probably, by this point, he had replayed the whole thing in his head a thousand times.

"But then you went to see her the night of her death?" Maya prompted him.

"I went round to make things up to her," J.D. said. "Bought her flowers, and I *never* used to get her flowers, unless you count the times that I'd take them out of the bayou. This was a big, expensive bunch, and... well, she'd had some time to think, too."

Maya could see the echo of the hope he'd had in his face.

"So what happened then?" Maya asked.

"We talked," J.D. said. "I haven't ever been good at talking, and I guess... well, I guess we got out of the habit. I told her that sleeping with someone was a mistake, that I regretted it ever since. We talked about the way our relationship was going, and if I was serious about her. I was going to get a proper job, something where I would drive down to Alexandria every day, not just whatever I could pick up. And... well, honestly, I don't think either of us could imagine not being together like that. I loved her, and she loved me."

Maya nodded to herself. That fit with what Samantha's mother had said about her calling to say that she was taking J.D. back. More than that, she couldn't see any evasive behaviors on his face, no deviation from the pattern of physical behavior he'd established. As far as Maya could see, he was telling the truth.

"So then what happened?" Maya asked.

56

"Then I left," J.D. said. "I mean, we still weren't made up enough that I was going to stay the night, you know? So I headed home, but went by a store to grab some things on the way. Drove all the way to Alexandria to do it. I swear, I left, and she was fine. Then when I came back in the morning…"

"Why did you come back in the morning?" Maya asked. This was another part of his story that she could imagine Sheriff Recks latching onto. He'd left, but then come back and found the body? It was simpler, easier to believe, that he'd killed her and sat there all night trying to work out what to do before coming up with the plan to call it in and pretend that he'd found the body.

"Because I wanted to fix Samantha breakfast," J.D. said. "I thought it would be a good surprise. Romantic. I had my key. I figured I'd cook, then take it up to her, then…"

"Then you'd get the make-up sex you missed out on the night before?" Maya guessed.

"Well… kind of, yes."

Yes, that was pretty much the kind of guy she was dealing with. The kind who thought that a few gifts were enough in a relationship, and everything was fine again. But being a bad boyfriend wasn't a crime, or several of Maya's exes would be in here with J.D.

"That's why I went to the store the night before," he said. "I wanted something fancy, I wanted to show her that I'd changed."

"So you went there the next morning and you found the body," Maya said.

His eyes took on a haunted look. "She was… just lying there, blood all around her. I ran over to try to help, and I got blood all over me before I realized that I couldn't do anything. I just… stood there, for so long. Then I called the cops. Worst decision of my life."

Except that if he'd run, he would have looked twice as guilty. The only question was whether he looked guilty to Maya now. Could it have been him? Honestly, her instincts said no. He wasn't a great guy, and it sounded as though he'd been a worse boyfriend, but neither of those things made him guilty. To Maya, it looked more and more as though he'd just been someone convenient for the local PD to get a result.

"Did you see any sign of anyone else there?" Maya asked.

J.D. shook his head.

"What about anything out of place? Anything that shouldn't have been there?"

"I just saw her, lying there," J.D. said.

"Well, was there anyone who might have a reason to kill Samantha?" Maya guessed he'd have thought about that one a lot, while he'd been in here.

"Everyone loved her," J.D. said. "*I* loved her."

Maya realized that she wasn't going to get much else.

"Thank you, J.D. you've been very helpful," Maya said, standing.

"So that's it?" J.D. said. "I thought you said you wanted to help me."

"I do, but to do that, I need proof. I'll keep looking into it all."

She needed more than one conversation to overturn his conviction. She wasn't even certain that he hadn't done it. All she had to go on was her nagging feeling that there was a lot more to this than a jilted boyfriend.

She headed back out, retrieving her service weapon from the guard at the reception and heading back to her rented car. Maya was almost there when she saw the trouble that was waiting for her.

Sheriff Recks was leaning against her car, and he didn't look happy.

58

CHAPTER ELEVEN

Maya couldn't think of a way to avoid the sheriff, so she got ready for the confrontation that seemed sure to follow. She forced herself to smile, in spite of the scowl on the sheriff's face.

"Sheriff Recks, come to help me with my investigation?"

"What are you doing here?" the sheriff demanded. "I thought you'd take one look at the file and take your pretty little self home. Instead, I get a call from the prison saying you're here asking questions."

So the sheriff had friends in the prison. That was good to know.

"I'm here to speak to your suspect," Maya said.

"J.D. isn't a 'suspect;' he's a convicted felon. Judge and jury agreed that he did this. Last I heard, that's how the law in this country works."

The sheriff stopped leaning on Maya's car and took a step forward, moving into her space, the bulk of him making him physically intimidating. He was probably hoping that Maya would take a step back. Instead, she put a hand on his chest lightly and moved him out of the way as she stepped around to her car.

She realized that she was half hoping that he would try something in that moment, if only for the excuse to show him that she wasn't so easy to mess with. She was getting caught up in his macho bullshit, but it was hard not to rise to the bait.

"We'll see," Maya said. "Right now, I'd say the jury's out on J.D., and on how good a job you did by bringing him in."

"Now listen," Sheriff Recks said. "I don't want you messing all this up. If you know what's good for you, you'll get away from my prison, get on a plane, and go home."

Maya took a deep breath to keep her rising anger in check. She didn't like the sheriff trying to bully her like this, and her instinct with bullies was always to head straight into the confrontation. If it went too far, though, that might be the excuse the sheriff needed to get her out of there.

"The last I heard, Sheriff, this prison was the property of the federal government. That's the same federal as in Federal Bureau of

Investigation. If anyone's in the wrong place here, it's you. Now, excuse me, I have an investigation to conduct."

For a moment, it looked as though the sheriff might try to block Maya's way to her car. She tensed for the possibility, frankly almost welcoming it. The sheriff must have seen some of that, though, because he took a step back.

"Don't say I didn't warn you," he said.

Maya ignored him and drove off. It was getting late, and she needed to find a hotel.

*

Rather than trying to find a place to stay in Pollock, Maya drove the twenty minutes back to Alexandria. It was getting into evening now, and even though her instinct was to make as much headway on the case as possible, it had been a long flight over, and the trip to the prison had taken up time. It was probably better to start again tomorrow.

Maya headed up to her room, which was as basic and standard as every other hotel room she'd been in. The same bed as everywhere else, the same chair, the same décor. She tried to relax a little, but she found it hard to do, pacing, then grabbing coffee.

The confrontation with the sheriff was a big part of it. It wasn't just that it he was so obviously hostile, it was the way his obstruction was likely to slow her down working the case. She only had a week to find her answers, and if Maya had to spend half of that time arguing with the sheriff, then the time might disappear right out of her grasp.

She found herself longing for the kind of help that she'd had from Detective Spinelli on the last case, and that took Maya a little by surprise. She was used to working alone. She *enjoyed* working alone, with no one else to have to watch out for. Yet now, she found herself wishing that she could just talk the case through with him, bounce ideas off him.

Then it occurred to her that she could, and in that moment the desire to talk to Marco was almost overwhelming. Taking out her phone, she called him, and was glad to hear his voice on the other end of the line.

"Maya, is everything all right?" he asked.

"Yes, sorry. I'm on another case, and… honestly, I just need someone to talk to about it."

60

"I can do that," Marco said. Just like that, no questions. "What's happening there? Actually, I suppose that's the first thing. Where is *there*?"

"Louisiana," Maya replied. "I'm currently in a Best Western in Alexandria, but the actual case is in Pollock. Another one from the kidnapper."

"With another deadline?"

"A week this time," Maya replied. "We don't know who he'll kill if I fail, but we've already had a… warning after my department tried another raid."

The thought of the pictures the kidnapper had sent, detailing every injury he'd inflicted on someone because of her, made her feel sick.

"They tried that *again*?" Marco said. "After how badly last time went?"

"I couldn't stop them." That wasn't the thing Maya wanted to talk to him about. "Look, is it ok to talk to you about this case? I don't want to think that I'm interrupting you while you're chasing down perps of your own."

"At this time of the evening?" Marco replied. "Not all of us work all night until we catch the bad guy, Grey. Besides, I'm taking a little time off after everything that just happened with the Postmartin case."

"You've earned it," Maya said. He'd been working the Anne Postmartin case for the two years since her death.

"But it also means that I have plenty of time to listen to what's going on with your case. So what's happening there? What's the new case?"

"A woman called Samantha Neele, a corrections officer here in Pollock. She was killed eighteen months ago. Her boyfriend found the body, and the local cops decided that it was him because they'd broken up the day before. They decided that they argued, he tried to get her back, she rejected him, and he killed her. He was convicted of it."

"Convicted?" Marco said. "So the case is closed?"

"The FBI file was never closed."

"There's an FBI file?"

Maya tried to get her thoughts in order, and maybe that was a good thing. Having to explain it to someone else meant that she had to get the facts straight for herself.

"Samantha was killed on the night of the full moon," Maya explained, and she knew that would be enough. "The team looking for

61

the Moonlight Killer looked at the case, but it was a different MO, a stabbing."

"That's... a second case in a row with that connection?" Marco said.

"Maybe," Maya said. "I'm not sure if it was him, though."

"And the boyfriend?"

"I'm not sure about him, either." Maya tried to put her reasons into words. "Samantha's mother told me that her daughter called her the night of the murder. She said that they were getting back together. If that's the case, then suddenly the boyfriend's motive goes out of the window, right?"

There was a brief moment of silence, presumably as Marco thought.

"It does sound like he wouldn't have a reason, but that's not enough to overturn a conviction."

"I know," Maya said. "I went to talk to him. He says he went out to get groceries because he wanted to make her breakfast. Then, when I came out, the local sheriff was waiting for me. He really doesn't want me here."

"So you're there trying to solve all this without any help?"

"I can handle it," Maya said.

"I don't doubt it. What's your next move?"

Maya tried to think. The problem right now was that she had no context for all this. All she knew was what was in the file. She tried to think of the way she'd begun with Marco on the Postmartin case.

"I think I want to see where the crime happened. After that, well, I'll work it out from there."

*

Maya had to wait until the next morning before she went over to Samantha Neele's old place. To her surprise, the building was still empty, even after all this time. The combination of an out of the way place and the knowledge of the murder seemed to have discouraged anyone from buying it. The door was unlocked, which suggested that either the sheriff's department hadn't been careful about securing the place when they left, or local kids had been in to look around the place where the murder happened.

The house was small and wooden framed, raised up enough to avoid the possibility of flooding. As she stepped inside, Maya took in the musty smell of somewhere that hadn't been touched in years. She guessed that Samantha's mother owned the place now, so maybe she hadn't been able to bring herself to do anything with it?

Either way, it meant that Maya could walk through the crime scene. Taking out the case file, she looked through the photographs, trying to find the exact spot where Samantha Neele had been killed. Yes, she would have been here, just at the doorway to the kitchen, visible from the front door.

Maya looked around, taking in the back door, the basic layout of the house. The floor was wooden, and there was a dark stain on it where it had proven impossible to get the blood out. Maya looked around, trying to imagine what it might have been like.

The report said a single stab wound, and no obvious defensive wounds. That meant that Samantha had been caught by surprise. She would have seen someone entering through the front, and if J.D. had come in holding a knife, Maya had to believe that she would have reacted. The more she thought about it, the less she liked him as a suspect.

The only question was how she could prove it. The coroner's report said that Samantha had died sometime between eleven and midnight, certainly no later, but that didn't seem like enough. She could think of another way, though. Quickly, she called Samantha's mother.

"Did you want something else, Agent?" Ms. Neele asked.

"Just one thing," Samantha said. "What time did your daughter call you to say that she was getting back together with J.D.?"

"Pretty late," Ms. Neele said. "I think it was 11:45."

"You're sure?" Maya needed her to be certain about this if it was going to work.

"It was the last conversation I ever had with my daughter," Ms. Neele replied. "I remember it perfectly."

"Thank you," Maya said. As soon as she hung up, she made another call, this time to Deputy Director Harris.

"Grey, how are things going down there?"

"I have a potential starting point," Maya said. "But I need to check some financial records for a Johnathan Dennis, of Pollock, Louisiana."

"The one convicted of the murder?" Harris said.

"That's right. I need to know about his transactions on the night of the murder. Specifically, any made late that night."

"All right," Harris said. "I'll have someone check. Give me a few minutes."

He hung up, and all Maya could do was wait. Five minutes later, Harris rang her back.

"I have the transactions now. The last one seems to be from an all-night store in Alexandria."

"What time, sir?" Maya asked. That was the crucial question.

"Ten to midnight. Why?"

The pieces slotted into place, and Maya smiled.

"Because I think we've just established that Johnathan Dennis *couldn't* have been Samantha Neele's killer."

CHAPTER TWELVE

Maya was polite as she walked into the sheriff's office with the casefile they'd given her under her arm. She wanted to be calm, and reasonable, and polite about this. It was about doing this in the way that was best for the case, not about some personal satisfaction.

She even waited in line, behind a couple of drunks being brought in for fighting in the town's only bar. She didn't want to give the older deputy staffing the desk an excuse to tell her to leave. So she waited, and made her way forward, and even ignored the look of distaste on the face of the deputy when she got up in front of the desk. It was worse than the last time she'd been here.

"Are you still in town?" the deputy asked her, demonstrating the powers of observation that had probably gotten him where he was. There wasn't even an attempt to be polite about it.

Maya thought about the best way to do this. She considered the small size of the place. The main office was well within earshot, so she raised her voice slightly. "I'm here to see Sheriff Recks."

"What does *she* want?" Sheriff Recks's voice boomed from the next room, the anger in his voice palpable. Maya smiled at the thought that he'd probably been listening in from the moment she stepped into his station. She shouldn't really have taken that kind of enjoyment from him getting upset, but honestly, it was hard not to after the way he'd been with her during her time in Pollock so far.

"I'll go through, shall I?" Maya said to the deputy at the reception desk. "I think your boss wants to talk to me."

Without waiting for an answer, she walked past, into the office beyond. Sheriff Recks was already on his feet there, red faced and angry.

"What do you think you're doing now?" he demanded. He took an angry step towards her. "Why are you still looking at all this?"

"Because I have a job to do," Maya replied. She took a seat in front of his desk without waiting for him to ask. Ok, so it was confrontational, but it seemed *less* confrontational than just standing

65

there while he advanced on her. Besides, at some point, she had to stand up for herself with the locals, or they would never cooperate.

"What job? We caught the killer more than a year ago!"

He was still insisting on that, with no hint that he might be wrong, or that there might be a reason that Maya was investigating there in his town.

"No," Maya said. "You didn't. You put an innocent man away."

The sheriff looked just about angry enough to burst in that moment. He strode over behind his desk, but he didn't pick his chair up to sit on it. Instead he leaned over it, invading Maya's space. She found herself wondering if the attempt at intimidation was deliberate, or if it was just something he did with everyone around him. Then again, it didn't exactly make it better either way.

"Are you accusing us of not doing our jobs?"

It would be so easy to say yes, because they clearly hadn't. They'd obviously jumped at the first hint of a suspect and then ignored anything that didn't fit. For now, though, Maya didn't say it that way. She needed the sheriff to listen, not just argue with her. This would all go better if she could get him to see things her way.

That was the ideal. If she could come in here and show Sheriff Recks that he needed her help to catch the real killer, then maybe, just maybe, he might start to be helpful. With that in mind, Maya put the case file down on his desk.

"I've added a few things," Maya said.

"What kind of things?" The sheriff still hadn't made any attempt to pick up his chair and sit down. He was still looming over Maya, as if she hadn't ever had a man try that before. She'd had far worse in the army.

"Most importantly, a timeline of that night, including J.D.'s movements. At just before midnight, the time the coroner says Samantha was murdered, he was in Alexandria, trying to set up some big romantic gesture to thank her for taking him back."

Sheriff Recks was already shaking his head. He clearly didn't like this. He'd probably repeated the story of that night to himself so often by now that it had become an unalterable truth in his mind.

"That's... she broke up with him. There was no way that she would take a scumbag like that back."

"A scumbag?" Maya said, even though it was pretty much what she'd thought of J.D. too.

66

"Do you know how many times I've seen him through this station?" the sheriff asked. "Do you know all the stuff I've heard he's been involved in that we could never quite prove? He's a criminal. There's no way *anyone* would take him back, let alone a corrections officer."

One of the things that Maya had learned when it came to the psychology of crimes was that it was important to know where the limits of it lay. Understanding people could help with guessing their motivations, but when that understanding met the facts and didn't fit, it wasn't the facts that you ignored.

"Samantha's mother told me that she called her to say she was doing exactly that."

Maya could see the sheriff trying to think, obviously trying to come up with ways to refute what she was saying. He didn't think for long, but then, from what Maya could see, that had been his problem throughout this case.

She saw him pick up the case file, flicking through it rapidly, obviously hunting for something that he'd half remembered. Maya was surprised that he hadn't read through every detail the moment she'd come into town.

"The coroner's report says that Samantha Neele was killed between 11pm and midnight," Sheriff Recks said, with a look of triumph. "Plenty of time for J.D. to have gotten over to Alexandria."

Maya had been expecting him to say something like that. He didn't know the rest of it, because he'd never bothered to ask about the rest of it. He'd found what he'd thought was an answer, and not gone any further.

"Now read the timeline," Maya countered. "That phone call I told you about from Samantha to her mother? Her mother says it happened at a quarter to midnight. She was still alive then."

"So maybe she's wrong about the time." Sheriff Recks clearly wasn't going to let it go that easily.

Maya could understand someone getting attached to their pet theories, but this seemed like too much. Ms. Neele was wrong? About something like that?

"Do you honestly think she is?" Maya asked, but she hadn't left it up to chance anyway. She'd checked. "Look at the next page. Phone records for the number are right there. However much you might dislike J.D., however much of a criminal he may or may not be, your suspect isn't the killer."

In another man, that might have brought a moment of realization, maybe even an apology, but it seemed that Sheriff Recks wasn't that man. His expression only hardened.

"I told you before," Sheriff Recks said. "J.D. isn't a suspect, he's a convict. Tried and found guilty by a jury. We did our jobs right."

Maya couldn't help herself, then. "You did your jobs terribly. You took the easy win, and because of that an innocent man has been in jail for eighteen months. I went to visit him the other day, and he was broken by prison. He's never going to be the same again."

"I'm supposed to feel sorry for a killer?" the sheriff snapped at her.

"You were supposed to do your job!" So much for any attempt to be polite and reasonable about this. The sheriff had made that more or less impossible anyway, though. "You were supposed to look at all the evidence. You obviously didn't look at Samantha's phone records, or talk to her mother properly."

"We interviewed the Neeles," Sheriff Recks insisted.

"And what? *Told* them that you'd gotten the killer in custody? Sold them on your version of events so that they didn't want to add in anything that didn't seem relevant?"

Sheriff Recks picked up his chair then and set it back in place.

"Whatever you say, whatever you do, J.D. has still been convicted of this. You think you can convince a jury otherwise?"

"Yes," Maya said simply. "In fact, my bosses are already doing it. Deputy Director Harris will be putting this evidence in front of a judge today, and I fully expect Johnathan Dennis to walk free."

"You're letting a killer out of jail?"

"I'm freeing an innocent man," Maya snapped back, standing now. "If you wanted the killer behind bars, then you should have found him, rather than jumping at the first suspect you saw."

She didn't wait for the sheriff's reply, but picked up the case file and walked out. Maya could see that she wasn't going to convince him, and every moment she spent trying was another second ticking off the clock towards her deadline.

She headed out to her car, and tried to calm down. She was a little surprised by just how angry she felt right then, just how much the sheriff's incompetence had managed to get under her skin. Except it wasn't just that; it was a whole raft of things about him. It was the way he behaved towards her, trying to intimidate her in a way Maya suspected he wouldn't have tried with a male agent. It was the fact that he wouldn't listen, and wasn't prepared to change his mind even when the evidence told him that he should. It was, frankly, just about everything about his department, which seemed to be about as small town and parochial as it was possible to get.

Why was the sheriff so attached to the idea of J.D. as the killer? Was it really just about him being up for re-election in his post? Maya supposed that people did worse for less. She'd *seen* them do worse, but had he really thought that she would stop her investigation so that he wouldn't look bad? That wasn't down to her. He'd done that himself.

Maya just had to hope that he wouldn't take the antagonism any further. She'd already used up a day, and the last thing she needed was more interference from the sheriff's department.

For now, though, Maya did her best to put him from her mind. She needed to focus on the case, and on what came next. She'd succeeded in freeing an innocent man, but that wasn't going to be enough to satisfy the kidnapper.

It wasn't enough to satisfy Maya, either. She needed to find real answers in this case, and that meant looking at the avenues that hadn't been explored. That meant just about everything, given the way the sheriff's department had investigated.

One avenue stood out, one connection to her previous case. It was one that the original FBI team had dismissed quickly, but that link made Maya want to take it more seriously. At least to ask a few questions and consider the possibility.

She needed to find out if this was actually the work of the Moonlight Killer.

CHAPTER THIRTEEN

The first thing Maya did with the Moonlight Killer angle was to ask around town, to see if the rumor mill there had any reason beyond the date of the killing to link the crime to the serial killer.

Ordinarily, she might have asked the local police about something like this, but after everything that had happened with the sheriff, Maya suspected that wasn't an option.

She had other things she wanted to know too. Maya wanted to know more about who Samantha Neele had been, what she was like, who her friends and her acquaintances were. If there was any advantage to working in a town this small, it had to be that everyone knew everyone else's business, right?

She started at the diner, on the basis that everyone who lived in the town would probably pass through there sooner or later. The waitress looked as if she'd worked there for years. She was serving an older couple, but came over when Maya waved her across.

"Hey," she said. "Did Samantha Neele used to come in here?"

The waitress frowned. "Why do you want to know about her? Didn't you hear she died? That no good ex of hers killed her."

Maya flashed her badge. "No, he didn't. We just found evidence proving it, and now we're going to have to look at every other aspect of her life to find out what really happened. I take it you knew her…"

"Vivian. I knew her. She used to come here after work sometimes, when she was too dead tired to cook. Used to say that working at the prison was the hardest job in the world, and the best. You're serious about it not being J.D.?"

"Everyone knows it was the Moonlight Killer!" the man from the older couple called out. Ordinarily, Maya might have been worried about people overhearing so much, but here, it was useful.

"What makes you think it was the Moonlight Killer?" she asked.

"It was on the night of the full moon, wasn't it?" the older man demanded.

"Now, Henry, not everyone wants to hear your conspiracy theories," the woman with him said.

70

"No, it's all right," Maya said. "I want to hear everything. Is there anything *other* than the date that makes you think it's him?"

"Isn't that enough?"

No, it wasn't, not by a long way. The Moonlight Killer always struck on the full moon, but that didn't make every murder, then, into one of his. Maya's last case had proved that much, and in this one, there was also the fact that Samantha Neele had been stabbed, whereas the Moonlight Killer favored strangulation when it came to killing his victims.

"Did you know Samantha?" Maya asked the couple.

"We saw her around," the woman said. "Nice girl. Always happy to help if you needed it. I asked her once what such a nice girl was doing working in a prison. She said she couldn't imagine doing anything else."

Maya could imagine saying the same thing when it came to her own job. It was easy for people to misunderstand tough jobs like theirs. People thought that they were something to do only for the money or because you couldn't do anything else. For Maya, though, her job was about making a difference, and she got the feeling that Samantha's had been for her, too.

"Can you think of anyone who might have wanted to hurt her?" Maya asked. "I know everyone thought it was J.D. but, now that we know it isn't him, is there anyone else she'd argued with? Anyone else who might have wanted to hurt her?"

"It's hard to think of anyone," the man said. "That's part of why it must be the Moonlight Killer. There was no reason for anyone normal to kill Samantha. The only thing that makes sense is some kind of serial killer picking her out as a victim."

"And why would he do that, Henry?" the woman demanded.

"There doesn't have to be a reason. It could have been random. That's what makes serial killers so dangerous."

Except that Maya knew most serial killers *didn't* pick their victims out at random, the way people sometimes thought. They had preferences, victim profiles they liked to target, motives behind what they did that made sense to themselves even if they didn't to anyone else.

Of course, part of what made the Moonlight Killer so frightening was that his patterns were so hard to understand. Beyond killing on the night of the full moon and favoring strangulation, it was hard to say much about who he liked to kill, where, or why.

Yet, in a way, did that mean that Henry here had a point? If there was no clear reason why anyone might have killed Samantha Neele, did it make sense to attribute it to someone whose reasons were anything *but* clear?

It was tempting, but it also felt like a leap without any evidence to back it up. Maya didn't need conjecture at this point: she needed an answer that she could back up with evidence.

"Do you happen to know who Samantha Neele's friends were around here?" she asked.

The waitress answered that one. "I guess the big one would have been Cindy Lowell. She lives a couple of streets over with her family. I can give you her address if you like."

"Please." Maya took the address and headed over.

*

When Maya knocked, the door was quickly answered by a woman in her thirties, much shorter than Maya and heavily pregnant. She was blonde haired, with a round face and glasses. She wore a brightly patterned dress that hung from her loosely.

Maya took out her ID card.

"Cindy Lowell? I'm Agent Grey, with the FBI. I was hoping I could talk to you about Samantha Neele."

"You want to talk about Sam?" Her face screwed up in confusion, as if she couldn't quite believe that someone might be there for that. "All right, come in. Please forgive the mess."

There were toys out all over the floor, enough to form a small obstacle course that they had to pick their way through in order to get to a sofa.

"My two eldest are at kindergarten now," Cindy said. "And another one on the way. But Wayne and I always wanted a big family. What about you? Do you have kids?"

Maya managed a smile. "It's just me."

Maya could just about manage to look out for herself. The idea of looking out for kids on top of that seemed slightly terrifying.

"What's all this about?" Cindy asked.

"I've been sent to reinvestigate the case," Maya said. She left out the circumstances under which she'd been sent, and exactly who had sent her. "I've uncovered evidence that suggests that J.D. didn't do it."

"That… that's good," Cindy said. She looked relieved. Judging by what Maya had heard about J.D. she was probably the only one who was. The reaction caught Maya's interest.

"You sound as though you liked J.D.," Maya said.

She saw Cindy cock her head to the side. "It's more that I never wanted to believe that he could do something like that. You're sure it wasn't him?"

"I'm sure."

Yes, Maya could definitely see the relief there on the other woman's face.

"That's good. That makes sense. J.D. was always a little wild, but there was never any harm in him, you know? And the idea that he would ever hurt Sam… it just never made sense. He was devoted to her."

Not so devoted that he would never cheat on her, but sure. She sounded very certain about it, which was a good thing. Maya needed someone who had been close to Samantha, someone who knew about her life.

"But now, I need to work out who *did* kill her," Maya said. "That means I need to know more about Samantha. What was she like? What did she like to do? What was going on in her life around that time?"

"With her hours off, she'd go walking out in the woods sometimes. I'd go along with her and try to keep up," Cindy said. "She liked to get out into the outdoors. She used to say that was one of the best things about living out here. We'd go into Alexandria sometimes."

"And did anything ever happen there that was unusual?" Maya asked. "Did she ever argue with anyone, or were there any signs that someone had a problem with her?"

People sometimes cut loose when they got into the city. It wasn't likely, but there was always the chance of problems there that didn't touch her life in Pollock.

"The only time I can think of was a long time before her death," Cindy said. "We ran into a guy in a bar, and he started to get aggressive. Afterwards, it turned out that he was a former inmate at the prison, and he didn't like drinking with a guard around. Even that was nothing."

73

"Do you know his name?" Maya asked, but Cindy shook her head. "Ok, I need to ask some fairly personal questions about Samantha now. Did she drink too much? Did she ever take drugs? Did she gamble?"

Cindy actually looked amused by all of that. "Trust me, if you knew Sam, you wouldn't think any of that. She'd drink if we were having a girls' night out, but not otherwise. As for the rest… just no. If she were taking drugs, it would have gotten her fired. She loved her job. It was her life."

Her life, the same way that her work with the FBI was Maya's. It was still faintly possible that all of this was the work of the Moonlight Killer, but if it wasn't, then Maya needed to look for answers in the place where Samantha had spent most of her time. A place where there were plenty of violent criminals who might be only too eager to take the chance to get revenge on a guard.

"Thank you," she said. "You've been very helpful."

She headed to her car, taking out her phone. The first thing she wanted to do was chase down the Moonlight Killer angle, and she knew one person who'd made it his job to learn as much as possible about the serial killer. Who hadn't been able to avoid it when an FBI team had been convinced that Anne Postmartin had been killed by him.

Maya could have done this another way, of course. She could have called up the FBI headquarters and asked for more information. She could have looked the files up in the FBI system and done the work of compiling them all herself. Maya didn't, for a few reasons.

One was that she'd seen how Deputy Director Harris reacted to mentions of the Moonlight Killer. If he thought there was even a chance that the serial killer was involved, he would probably push for Maya to run down that lead as far as she could take it, and she wasn't sure if there was enough time for that.

Another was that Maya wanted another human being's assessment of the situation, not just a cold hard statement of the facts. She needed someone she trusted, someone who knew the Moonlight Killer cases, and who could help her decide if this was real or not.

Finally, though, there was the simple fact that it was an excuse to call Marco again. Maya had to admit to herself that she liked hearing his voice. Besides he *had* offered to help.

She called him, and was pretty surprised when the call went straight to voicemail. Marco had said that he was taking a few days off, and would be around if she wanted to call, after all.

"Hi, Marco, it's me, Maya. I was hoping to talk over an aspect of the case with you. Do you know of any cases where the Moonlight Killer has stabbed his victim? Um… you might not be able to call me back straight away. I'm heading to the prison to talk to the other guards there and find out if there's anything connected to the place that might have something to do with Samantha Neele's death. Call me back, ok?"

Maya hung up and started to drive off. If there were answers anywhere about Samantha's death, it made sense to look for them at the focal point of her life. That meant that she was going to have to go back to USP Pollock.

CHAPTER FOURTEEN

Out in the forest, Maya stopped her car to make another call, of the kind she didn't want to make when there might be other people around. She didn't want anyone to be able to see her reaction.

She called Harris. It was a while before he picked up, which probably meant that he had the President on the other line, or something. Maya was willing to wait, though.

"Grey, calling again so soon? Does this mean that you've found something?"

"Just reporting in on my next steps, sir," Maya said. "And on how the sheriff reacted."

She felt Harris probably deserved a heads up about that, in case he ended up fielding a barrage of complaints from the locals.

"Not well, I take it?"

"He looked as though he might explode. Even when I put the evidence in front of him, he ignored it and insisted that Johnathan Dennis was the killer."

Just thinking about it made Maya angry all over again. Maybe some of that came out in her voice, because of what her boss said next.

"And you were at your tactful best, I take it?"

She could hear the amusement in Harris's voice.

"Some time after the third or fourth time he tried to intimidate me, I *might* have told him just how bad the policework was on the original case."

There was a brief pause on the other end of the line.

"Grey, as your superior, I think I'm meant to remind you at this point of the importance of cooperation with local police departments, and how much their information can bring to a case."

His voice was stern, but Maya could hear that the amusement was still there.

"But?" she said.

"But in this case, you're probably better off without them. Men like Sheriff Recks have no place in law enforcement. If a complaint comes, I'll deal with it."

Maya was suddenly very grateful that Harris was her boss and not the sheriff.

"How are things going with the judge?"

"It's already happened. Johnathan Dennis will walk later today or tomorrow."

That brought Maya a sense of relief that was quickly shattered by Harris's next words.

"Now, tell me about the Moonlight Killer angle."

Maya paused, caught by surprise that her boss knew about that side of things already.

"I was going to work it out, Grey," he said when she didn't reply. "That specialist team you asked me to look into, it turns out they were assigned to trying to catch him. Once I had that and the date of the murder, the connection wasn't hard to put together. So, are you looking into it?"

Maya could hear the eagerness there, and it was her worst fears about this moment being realized. Harris wanted this to be about the Moonlight Killer, just as he had with her last case.

"I'm looking, sir, but I'm also examining other areas of Samantha Neele's life."

"That's a non-answer, Grey. Does it look likely that the Moonlight Killer is involved?"

Maya tried to consider it. Could he be?

"Honestly, there's no way of knowing yet. But the specialist team shut their investigation down pretty quickly."

"Only because they thought the killer had been caught," Harris said. "There has to be a reason that the kidnapper is pointing us at these Moonlight Killer cases. I think he wants the Moonlight Killer caught."

"Maybe, sir," Maya said, although she had her doubts. "But the last case didn't turn out to be him, so I think I need to take other aspects of this one seriously too. Right now, I'm heading to the prison to talk to the staff there, and find out if Samantha Neele had any enemies because of her job."

"All right," Harris said. "You're right, the main thing is to solve this. There's a life hanging in the balance."

"Do we know whose yet?" Maya asked, both because she wanted to steer the conversation away from the Moonlight Killer and because any information that might help find her sister had to be a good thing.

77

"Forensics haven't come back with a DNA match yet. There are a couple of domestic terrorism cases taking priority."

That was always the difficult thing working cold cases in the FBI. People thought that Maya had nearly infinite resources at her disposal, but they forgot that there were plenty of high profile, urgent cases out there that her colleagues were investigating. All too often, that meant she had to wait.

"That's fine, sir."

"I'll call you when anything comes through. In the meantime, let me know if you find any further connection to the Moonlight Killer."

He hung up, leaving Maya to keep making her way towards the prison. With the time she'd spent on the call, she pushed up against the speed limit as she drove through the expanse of the national forest, the trees and occasional wetlands spreading out around her, greenery sprouting up out of it as far as the eye could see. Here and there were small tracks leading off, but it was mostly just a straight road down to the prison now, and...

...and there were flashing blue lights in her rearview mirror. Maya heard the siren as she made out the cop car, flashing her to pull over. Maya did it with a frustrated sigh. She was being pulled over? Really?

She turned off the engine and waited while one of the sheriff's deputies got out of the car. Maya didn't know this one, a young man in his twenties, slender and with a swagger to his walk. He took his time heading over to Maya's car. Maya lowered the window, waiting for him.

"License and registration," he said as he reached her.

Maya got them out slowly, handing them to him. He seemed to take all the time in the world about reading them.

"Do you know how fast you were going right then, ma'am?" the deputy asked.

"Agent."

"Sorry?" the deputy said.

"Agent, not ma'am. Agent Grey, with the FBI. You've stopped me in the middle of an investigation."

That didn't seem to make any difference to the deputy.

"Do you know how fast you were driving, Agent?"

Maya shrugged. "I might have been going one or two miles over the limit, maybe, but-"

"Four miles an hour over," the deputy corrected her.

"Four? You stopped me because I was over by four?"

It was the sort of thing that happened when cops had been given quotas to meet, or when they'd been told to look out for any opportunity to stop a particular person. Maya was willing to bet on which of those two it was.

"Four over is still breaking the law. I'm going to have to write you a ticket."

Maya could feel her annoyance building. "This is because I made your sheriff look bad, right? It's some of the most petty, small minded-"

"Are you refusing to take the ticket, ma'am?" the deputy asked.

Maya saw his hand straying down towards his holster. She understood what the point of this was then. It wasn't just to try to annoy her with a traffic stop. It was to try to get her to react, so that the deputy would have an excuse to arrest her and make her sit in a cell for however long it took Harris to get her out. Probably, the sheriff would hold her for as long as he could, and with a woman's life on the line if she didn't meet her deadline, Maya couldn't afford to let that happen.

So she smiled as sweetly as she could and held out her hand. "I'm happy to take it. Write me up, deputy."

He looked at her with a degree of hostility that suggested that he might try to arrest her in spite of her playing along with his little game. Maya could feel her adrenaline rising as she tried to decide what she would do if he did. Her instinct was to take him down, slap cuffs on him for trying to abuse his position, and hope that Harris could sort it all out.

Again, though, that would be time she didn't have.

Finally, though, the deputy reached for a pen and wrote her up a ticket. He held it out to Maya, but then let it drop, just short of her hand. Thankfully, she'd been expecting just such a disrespectful move, and caught it. If she hadn't, he'd have probably tried to write her up for littering.

"Thank you, deputy," Maya said, still affecting sweet contrition.

She didn't threaten, didn't argue, didn't do anything that would make all of this last even a moment longer. She waited for the deputy to return to his car and drive off, then punched the dashboard hard enough that her knuckles hurt.

A part of her wanted to call Harris again, report this harassment and try to get him to do something about Sheriff Recks. What could he do,

79

though? The sheriff kept or lost his job based on the elections for it. His competence for the role had almost nothing to do with it. Maya had to remind herself that in those terms, she already had the best revenge on the sheriff, because the suspect he'd managed to get convicted was about to walk free. That would make him look pretty bad in the eyes of the people who might vote for him. It might even be enough to see Pollock get itself a new sheriff.

Maya kept driving towards the prison, this time staying carefully under the limit, using her turn signals and her mirrors, being very careful not to give a waiting deputy anything that they could reasonably pull her over for. She pulled up in the parking lot of the prison, and headed for the entrance.

There, waiting for her, she saw Marco Spinelli.

The Cleveland detective looked as amazing as he always did, with his leanly muscled swimmer's body that towered over even Maya, his slightly disheveled good looks, the jacket that had seen better days over slacks and… yes, he was wearing the cowboy boots that he'd put on for a joke back in Cleveland. Maya didn't want to have to tell him that she currently didn't have the best impressions when it came to sheriffs. His dark hair was just starting to get out of control, and he ran a hand through it as Maya approached, as if suddenly aware of his appearance.

The wave of joy that hit her at the sight of Marco was surprising in its intensity. It wasn't just that it was Marco, and Maya could happily have looked at him all day. It was, simply, that she needed someone there right then. She needed to feel as if she wasn't alone in all this, set against both the case and the sheriff's department.

Now, right when she needed him, Marco was here.

"How?" Maya said, as she came closer. "How are you here?"

"I told you I had some days off," Marco said. "So when I heard all about this case, I knew I had to be here for you. I want to help. I want to make sure that you get your sister back. Your boss is ok with it. I checked."

That meant more to Maya than she could put into words. The thought that Marco would do that for her, without even being asked… it was a lot.

"But how are you *here*?" Maya asked, gesturing to the prison.

"I got your message as I was getting off my flight in," Marco said. "I hired a car and came straight here. I figured I'd probably be waiting for you to come back out. Something slow you down?"

80

"Just the local sheriff's department being obnoxious," Maya said. Right then, though, that mattered far less than it had. Marco was here, and now it felt as though she had backup, whatever happened.

"So, *why* are we here?" Marco asked.

"I want to know more about Samantha Neele's life as a prison guard," Maya said. "I want to know who she worked with, who she guarded, and who might have a grudge against her."

And maybe, just maybe, who might have been the one to sneak into her house to kill her that night.

CHAPTER FIFTEEN

Frank sat in his cabin, watching the news. Up here, he couldn't keep track of things in the detail that he did below ground, couldn't risk being seen, because even out here in the middle of nowhere there was a chance.

He would hate to have to kill someone he hadn't planned to. That would be… disorderly, imprecise, not part of the plan for all this.

But in this case, he could get all the information he needed just from watching the right news channels. He watched the young reporter on the screen, dressed so seriously, her hair and makeup worked on until she almost shone from the screen. He couldn't help thinking that, for appearance, at least, she would make a great bunny for him.

But it wasn't just about appearance for him. A man with such unsophisticated tastes was easily caught.

"A Louisiana man will be released tomorrow after serving nearly two years for a crime he didn't commit," the reporter said. "I'm standing outside the courtroom in Alexandria where today, the near half decade old conviction against Johnathan Dennis for the murder of his partner Samantha Neele has been overturned. The release comes as the FBI have reinvestigated the case, finding flaws in the original case produced by the Pollock Sheriff's Department."

Frank felt a moment of satisfaction as he heard those words. Not at the thought of a man being set free; he didn't care one way or the other about the fate of Samantha Neele's boyfriend. Instead, the satisfaction was at the thought that he had done this. He had brought this about with the control he had over Agent Grey thanks to her sister and the rest.

Now, it just remained to be seen what else she would do for him. He'd sent her a lock of hair to encourage her along with the photographs. He found himself wondering how long it would be before she got the results of that. Hopefully not too soon. It would be more interesting later in the case.

Frank headed down into his bunker, putting on his mask, taking up his stun gun and heading through to the complex of rooms where his bunnies waited. After what he'd done to one of their number, they scattered at his approach, but he would not allow that.

"Gather," he called out. "The main room. Now."

He went through to that room, taking the only chair there and waiting while they came in, moving with all the fear and readiness to scatter of their namesakes. They were lovely in their way, his bunnies. Well, all except the one he'd marred to make a point, but even that had a kind of beauty to it. Frank had made her into a work of art. More than that, he'd made her useful, giving the FBI the only kind of warning they would understand.

One by one, his bunnies sat around by his feet, in their allotted places. Where before some had started to almost accept their confinement, now, they all looked terrified. The one he'd beaten moved slowly with it, looking more frightened than all the rest. Frank stood and moved to her. She flinched back automatically.

"Stay," he commanded her. "Absolutely still. If you move, I will know."

She froze in place.

Frank went to fetch a small medical kit and started to tend the worst of her injuries with iodine and gauze. In truth, it didn't take much more than that, because he had been very careful in the damage he had inflicted. He *had* to be careful, or he would have to find a new bunny to replace this one. He needed all of them if he was going to get dear Maya to do everything that he needed her to do.

He talked as he worked, speaking to the one he tended, but making it loud enough that the others could hear as well.

"You'll be glad to know that dear Maya is making progress with the task I have given her. Why, today, she found proof that a man who had been convicted of murder was not the one who committed the act. He will walk free, thanks to her."

"Will we?" the bunny asked in a small voice.

Frank touched the side of her face tenderly. Because of the bruises, that probably hurt as much as if he'd slapped her.

"That is not the game, not the *point*. Who cares if one stupid man goes free, if she does not find the whole truth? When she finds *that*, I will free one of you, not before. Do you think that she will?"

The bunny didn't say anything for several seconds. She seemed too frightened to do so.

83

"Answer me," Frank snapped, and he could see the tears forming at the corners of her eyes. "Answer!"

"Yes, yes, I think she'll do it. She did it before," the bunny said in a small voice.

"She was late, before," Frank reminded her. "Which reminds me."

He took a digital count down from his pocket. It was nowhere near as large as the one in the bunker's control room, but this time it didn't need to be. It was better if they *all* saw the countdown, all saw the time ticking away as dear Maya struggled to solve her case.

Frank had given her enough time for this one. He wouldn't be as lenient as he had been last time around. Carefully, precisely, he set the countdown on the chair that he had occupied.

"I want Maya to find the killer," Frank said. "I want her to find the truth. But if she fails… well, you see how much time you all have before one of you dies, bunnies. I suggest that you might want to start saying your goodbyes."

Frank could see the panicked looks on their faces. They didn't know yet which of them it would be, and that uncertainty would bring the right kind of fear to all of them.

Maya didn't know either. All she knew was what Frank wanted her to know: that she had to do what he wanted, or one of the women here would pay the price.

CHAPTER SIXTEEN

As she headed into the prison, Maya was grateful that she had Marco with her. She hadn't realized quite how much she'd come to rely on him in just a few short days, and now it meant more than she could say that he was there to watch her back.

Of course, watching *him* was hardly a chore, either.

They went in together, and Maya was glad to see that there was a different guard on the front desk, a heavily built man in his late twenties, with sandy hair and a ruddy complexion.

"Can I help you?" he said.

"Agent Grey, FBI. This is Detective Spinelli, who's consulting with me." Maya didn't add that Marco was with the Cleveland PD, because she didn't need the questions about his jurisdiction. "I was here yesterday to talk to Johnathan Dennis."

"The guy who's getting released tomorrow? I heard about that. It's pretty horrible to think that the guy has been locked up here for so long, and… well, people weren't exactly kind to him."

"Because you thought he killed one of your own?" Marco said.

"Yeah." The guard looked a little uncomfortable then. "And now it turns out that he didn't even do it."

Maya nodded, trying not to think of everything that must have happened to J.D. in here. Prison was hard enough, but prison when the guards actively hated you for what they thought you'd done had to be ten times worse. No wonder he'd looked so broken when she'd spoken to him.

"Now," she said, "I need to find out who *really* killed Samantha. That's why I'm back here."

"You want to talk to Dennis again?"

"Actually, yes," Maya said, although that hadn't been her intention when she'd set off. Maybe now that he knew that she was serious about helping, he might remember something more. He might have thought of something since the last time they'd spoken. "But not straight away. I'd rather talk to you and the other guards, if that's ok?"

"I guess so," the guard said. "If you want to talk to me, we'll have to do it here, because I'm not allowed to leave the front desk. You'll probably find a couple of others in the guards' break room, over that way."

Maya decided to start with this guard, since at least he was a lot friendlier than the one she'd run into the last time she was here.

"So, who are you?" Maya asked.

"Don," the guard replied. "Don Gravewood. I've been working here pretty much since I got out of school."

"So you knew Samantha Neele?"

Maya saw him nod.

"She always looked out for me. Well, for all of us, really. There are some guys, they just get through their shift and don't really care about anything or anyone beyond that, but Samantha always made an effort. Someone needed help moving, Samantha was there. Someone wasn't feeling well, Samantha would cover for them."

"Did making an effort include with the prisoners?" Marco asked.

"*Especially* with the prisoners. A lot of the guards get so… toughened up by it all after a while that they forget they're guarding people. Samantha never did that."

That was the second time Maya had heard that. It made her wonder about the prisoners in question.

"So, how many of the prisoners here would have known her?" she asked.

"Probably every inmate knew her name," Don said.

"And did any of them get close to her?" Maya asked.

She saw Don frown at that.

"Are you asking if any of them fraternized with her? Because that just wouldn't happen. Samantha knew the limits, and she was careful."

"*She* knew the limits," Maya said, echoing his words, "but what about the prisoners. Were there any who wanted to get closer to her? Any who might have taken it personally when she told them no?"

It was possible, wasn't it? A prisoner who thought that he had a special connection with his guard, and that turned to anger when he found out that it wasn't reciprocated the same way? A prisoner who had gotten out and maybe tried to make a pass at Samantha? Maybe he'd even heard that she'd broken up with J.D. and come over to try to suggest being with her, then stabbed her when she'd rejected him.

86

It was a lot to assume, but Maya had definitely seen stranger things in the course of her career.

"There were a few guys who would make jokes, but nobody serious that I knew about. You'd have to ask some of the other guards."

"I will," Maya said. "What about the opposite? Were there any prisoners who made threats? No matter how good she was with the inmates, Samantha was still a guard."

"I mean… obviously," Don said. "We all get threats. You work the maximum security wings, and half the guys in there will hurt you if you give them a chance. But there's a gap between that and going out when you get out to kill one of the guards."

Maybe, or maybe not. With so many dangerous people around, it seemed obvious that one of them might have been the killer. It was just a question of narrowing it down.

"Was there anyone specific?" she asked.

"Not that I know of," Don said. "One of the other guards might know more."

"Thank you," Maya said. "Which way to the break room?"

"Just through there, then third door on the left."

Maya noticed that he didn't ask them for their weapons, the way the guard the other day had. Maybe he was just more lax about his job, but Maya suspected that it might also have been that guard trying to mess with her, to show her who was boss.

She and Marco headed through to the break room. It was a small, largely empty space, with a few chairs, a couple of tables, and a small kitchen area where they could prepare food if they wanted. There were a couple more guards in there, and she recognized one of them instantly, because it was the shaven headed guard from the other day.

"What are you doing back here?" he asked.

"Conducting an investigation," Maya replied. "I didn't catch your name yesterday."

"Because I didn't give it," the guard said.

Marco stepped up next to Maya. "I believe the agent asked you a question, friend."

This was one of the benefits of having backup, especially when that backup was as tall and muscled as Marco was. Maya saw the guard consider his options, then shrug.

"Wood. Jeremiah Wood. I'm the head guard here. What's it to you?"

87

"Nothing so far," Maya said. "You knew Samantha?"

"I worked with her. We all did."

"So you might have known if anyone wanted to hurt her?" Maya suggested.

Jeremiah snorted at that. "Look around you. A whole prison full of scumbags who'll put a shiv in you as soon as look at you. I heard you got the boyfriend off."

"Because he didn't do it," Maya said.

"Yeah, well, a guy like that, he's guilty of *something*. They all are."

It seemed like a very different approach to the one Samantha had taken.

"Did you and Samantha get on?" Maya asked him.

He shrugged. "Well enough. Work is work. I'm not here to make friends. You start putting your whole life into your work in a place like this, and suddenly it's over. Look at Samantha. Spent so much effort on trying to reform the inmates here, like any of them could be, didn't have any time left to live her life."

From what Maya had heard, Samantha had more than managed to live her life well alongside her job. She guessed that at least some of her colleagues didn't know her so well after all.

The frustrating part was that they didn't seem to know anything specific at all. Yes, both Don and Jeremiah had agreed that maybe some of the inmates might have wanted to hurt Samantha, but they hadn't been able to give Maya a name to go on. When she only had a week, she couldn't afford to trawl through every inmate who had gotten out, hoping to run into the one who had killed Samantha.

It was time to explore the other option there in the prison. She needed to talk to J.D. again.

*

Maya was pleased to see that they didn't bring J.D. to the interview room in shackles this time. He might still technically be a prisoner for another day, but it seemed that the guards were doing their best to make it more pleasant for him.

He definitely looked happier and more optimistic. He was walking straighter, as if the weight of his experience had been lifted off his shoulders. Maya knew it wouldn't be that simple, though. Even a short time inside a federal prison would have a lasting effect on anyone, and it would only be worse because, all that time, J.D. had known that he didn't deserve to be there.

Now, he was coming out into a world where his girlfriend was gone, and which had moved on without him. A world where plenty of people would probably still think that he had played some role in Samantha's death. For all that Maya was glad that she'd been able to prove he hadn't done this, the next steps would be anything but easy.

"You did it," J.D. said as he sat down at the table in the interview room. "You actually managed to get me out of here. I never thought anyone would."

"I'm glad I was able to help," Maya said. She gestured to Marco. "This is Detective Spinelli, a colleague of mine. We're trying to find out who actually killed Samantha. Is it all right if we ask you a few more questions?"

"Sure... I guess," J.D. said. "But I don't know what I can tell you both. I want to help. I want whoever did this caught, but it's not as if I *know* anything. I've been over that night a thousand times in my head, but there's nothing. No detail I spotted that might tell you anything."

"Sometimes people know more than they think," Maya said. "Besides, I'm not here to ask you about the night of the murder again."

"You're not?" J.D. looked confused by that, as if he couldn't work out why he was in the interview room if Maya didn't want to ask him about that night.

"I want to ask you if Samantha used to talk about her job," Maya said.

"Yeah, I guess so," J.D. replied. He seemed to think about it for a moment or two more. "Yeah, pretty often, really. She'd come home from work, and I'd ask her how her day had been and stuff. It was like she could really unload with me."

"So she talked about the prisoners she worked with?" Maya asked.

J.D. nodded at that. "Yeah, all the time. Samantha would always be talking about how someone was making progress or doing badly. I got pretty stressed whenever I heard she'd had to break up a fight or something, because I always thought she was going to be hurt, but she was tough, you know?"

Maya was starting to. She felt as though she was beginning to understand Samantha Neele pretty well.

"Did she ever talk about any prisoners who gave her any trouble? Maybe made threats?" Maya asked.

That took J.D. a little longer to answer.

"There was *one* guy. Really creeped Samantha out. A guy named Egan. Killed three people. Kept making comments about how Samantha would be number four."

That sounded promising, until Maya considered the obvious potential problem with a suspect like that. She hammered on the door for the guard.

"Ready to go already?" he asked.

"I actually have a question," Maya said. "There's a killer who was an inmate here, by the name of Egan."

"*Was*? He still is," the guard said. "Charlie Egan is serving life without parole. He's never getting out. And no, before you ask, there's no day release or work release for a guy like him. He's far too dangerous."

Which meant that he had the best possible alibi for the night of the murder. Maya felt a little deflated as that hit home. She'd thought she'd had a great idea, but then it had slipped away from her.

Except…

One part of it kept nagging at her: serial killers; and it took a moment or two for Maya to realize why.

"Marco," she said. "I think we're done here for now. J.D. when you get out of here, I might need to talk to you again."

"Whatever you need. You're the reason I'm getting out, after all."

Maya and Marco walked back out to the entrance. They got all the way outside before Marco stopped her.

"I've seen that look on your face before. You think you've got something, right?"

"We've been treating this case as if it's an isolated thing, because that's what the sheriff's department did. But what if it isn't? The killing was quick, neat, the way it would be if someone had done it before. They got into a house and killed a tough, capable prison guard without leaving any trace of themselves. That's not someone's first kill, is it, Marco?"

Marco shook his head. "Most murders are messy. Most people, even if they plan it, get things wrong. But what are you saying?"

Maya took a breath. "I think we're dealing with a serial killer."

CHAPTER SEVENTEEN

Maya had to force herself to stay under the speed limit as she and Marco rushed back to Alexandria, and went to the hotel Maya had booked. It seemed that Marco had managed to book a room in the same place, and Maya didn't know whether to be pleased or disappointed by that. The idea of having to share a room with him was... tempting.

She shook her head trying to focus on the case as she and Marco made their way to the hotel's dining room. Maya had her laptop with her, because if there was one advantage to staying in chain hotels across the country, it was the free WiFi. She watched as Marco tucked into the buffet there. For her part, Maya was too excited to eat.

"So you're sure it's a serial killer?" Marco said, as he started to work his way through a plate of potatoes.

"I'm not *sure*," Maya replied, because how was it possible to be sure about something like that unless someone was claiming a twisted kind of credit for it? "But you have to admit it makes sense. The neatness of the killing, the lack of evidence... it adds up."

"It could mean other things, too. It could point to some kind of military training, to having learned to kill there."

Maya considered that, but of the two of them, *she* was the one with the military background. She was the one who understood what that kind of trained individual would do, and more importantly, how.

"I don't think the MO is right," Maya said. "Most military personnel would favor a gun if they wanted to kill someone, and if it were a knife, then the way Samantha was killed is not the way it's taught to special forces."

Marco looked her over carefully. "You know that for a fact?"

"I... yes," Maya admitted. "I was attached to some of them back in the army. I had an interest in psychology even then, so I got pulled into units doing psyops, intelligence, that kind of thing."

"You must have seen a lot," Marco said.

Maya wasn't sure what to say to that. At the time, it had just seemed like what she had to do. In the midst of a firefight, or a dangerous mission, there had been no time to stop and think about the intensity of the situation.

"There were a few moments," Maya managed. She wasn't sure if she could go into all the details. She wasn't sure that she wanted to. There were always parts of the past that were better left alone.

To Maya's surprise, Marco didn't ask any more questions about that part of her past. The moment most people heard that Maya had been in the military, they usually wanted details of every little thing she'd done, every mission she'd gone on. Some of them asked because they had a hard time believing that Maya had done all that. Others just seemed to want to know it as some kind of entertainment.

Marco didn't, though. Instead, he gave her a look that suggested that he knew exactly how hard it was for her.

"So, a serial killer?" Marco said. "But not the Moonlight Killer?"

That was the other part of it. If Maya was so convinced that it was a serial killer, then why *couldn't* it be the Moonlight Killer?

"I don't know, Marco." Maya fired up her laptop and logged onto the FBI server. She didn't have local resources to rely on, but she still had the full records of the FBI at her disposal, along with all the help that Marco could give her. "It's a possible angle, but the MO really doesn't fit. And the Moonlight Killer isn't the only serial killer in the world."

"True, but scary." Marco had stopped eating now, obviously taking the whole thing more seriously. "The question is how we establish for sure if Samantha Neele was killed by one."

"We look for patterns," Maya said. "We find other murders that seem too similar to this one for it to be a coincidence. If there are enough, maybe details of those murders will help lead us to our killer."

Maybe there would even be suspects in other cases whose names wouldn't mean anything in isolation, but which would make more sense once she started to compare cases.

"Where do we start?" Marco asked. "Maybe with the details of the murder? If the MO is different enough that we don't think it's the Moonlight Killer, maybe it's enough to lead us to the real murderer."

It was a start, at least. Maya searched for deaths by stabbing, but almost immediately the problem with that became apparent. Stabbings? Across the whole of the country? Even over the course of a single year, it was thousands of cases, taking in everything from domestic violence to gang activity, random attacks by far right terror groups to drug runners trying to send a message.

It was overwhelming, and not just because of what it said about the chances of finding one killer among all of this. It was reminder that, however much Maya did, there was always more out there, more tragedy, more pain.

"Ok, so we need to narrow it down a little," Marco said.

"A *little*?" Maya wasn't sure if they would ever be able to narrow the field enough this way.

"What about people killed in their own homes?" Marco suggested. "By strangers who entered without being seen? There have to be fewer murders like that."

Maya put those details into the search too. Marco was right about it narrowing down the field. It eliminated all the files that were obviously domestic murders, all the ones where there was clear gang involvement. As tragic as those murders were, they weren't relevant here.

It still left too many. Maya couldn't go through all of them, couldn't hope to work through every file in time. The thought of not being able to solve this in time was almost too much. She couldn't help thinking of Megan, and what might happen to her if she was too slow this time. She found herself thinking about the pictures the kidnapper had sent, and the injuries he'd inflicted. Had that been on Megan? Even if it wasn't, *would* it be her next?

"Grey," Marco said. "*Grey,* are you ok?"

Maya shook her head, and Marco took her by the arm, helping her stand.

"It looks like you're having some kind of panic attack," he said. "Breathe slowly. Focus on my voice."

He walked with her around the dining room, leading her to the buffet.

"I couldn't eat," Maya said, as they reached it.

"And when did you *last* eat?" Marco countered.

"Diner. Earlier." Except that it had been a while ago now, and she'd barely eaten when she was there. The thought of finding an answer at the prison had propelled her through the door too quickly.

Marco looked worried for her, but there was also a stern note to his expression.

"You can't just keep running around flat out, chasing answers. You were close enough to crashing back in Cleveland, but now, you're trying to just roll through into the next case."

"It's not that," Maya insisted, although it was, at least a little. She felt so tired right then, like she'd been running back and forth as the kidnapper demanded, flat out from the start of all this. "He sent pictures, showing everything he'd done."

"You told me that," Marco replied, but then seemed to get it. "You're imagining him doing that to your sister?"

Maya nodded. It was impossible not to. Impossible to focus on anything else. It made even thinking about the case difficult.

Marco passed her a plate. "I still think you should eat something. If nothing else, it will give you something else to focus on for a few minutes."

"But we have to keep narrowing down the search." Maya didn't want to take a step away from it now, even though she couldn't see how they were going to get the numbers down to anything useful.

"Afterwards," Marco said, in a firm tone.

Maya wasn't the biggest fan of being bossed around. With most men, if they'd talked to her like that, she'd have reacted with an immediate retort. She wasn't the type to just meekly do what she was told. Yet now, Maya found herself going along with it, focusing on the food. Even putting it on her plate seemed to take an effort.

She ate alongside Marco, and with every bite, Maya longed to get back to the business of the case, but *not* thinking about it even for a few minutes seemed to be exactly what she needed right then. Slowly, Maya could feel her deep sense of panic at not being able to do enough to save her sister starting to subside.

"Feeling better?" Marco asked.

Maya nodded even though the fear for Megan wasn't about to go away.

"Then what do we need to do in order to narrow down the search?" Marco asked. "You know this, Grey."

Maya realized that she did, and probably Marco did too, given that he'd worked homicide.

"We need to use Samantha as a template for a victim profile," she said.

The first step was to limit the killings to only those that involved women. There were some killers who had a much broader victim

94

profile, but it was less common, and assuming that this killer only stalked women at least meant that they could eliminate a good portion of the potential cases.

What else did serial killers select their victims by? Looks, sometimes, but Maya didn't feel as though that was it here. Her instinct said that it might have more to do with Samantha's job as a prison guard.

She put that into the search, and now the number of files fell away rapidly. Female corrections officers being murdered was a rarity, but even so, there were three more cases in the files. The oldest stretched back six years, while one was as recent as eighteen months ago.

"There's actually a killer out there," Marco said. "You've found him."

"I want to check and make sure that this isn't coincidence."

Maya started to read the case files, one by one. Each one was chillingly similar. In each case, a female corrections officer had been found killed by stabbing, slain by someone who had entered their house quietly, without leaving a trace.

"It's one person," Marco said. "It has to be."

Maya nodded. "The trick now is to work out *who*."

There was only one way to do it that Maya could think of. Taking the names of the women, she started to look at the places where they'd worked. They'd been guards in correctional facilities around the country. Was it possible that anyone could have been in all those places?

Maya quickly found that there were men who had been in all of them, but only a handful, when the women had worked there. After all, it meant that there were men who were being arrested and tried in all corners of the country, rather than in their own back yard.

That number only fell when Maya realized the next part.

"It has to be someone who completed their sentence before the murder. If they were in prison, they couldn't have done it."

She focused on the release dates for the men in question, and the moment Maya did that, the list shrank to exactly one name: a man named Augustine Harmer, current residence...

"He lives in Shreveport, Marco. He actually lives near here."

"And he's the only one who's out who could have done it. He has to be the guy," Marco agreed.

Which meant that they suddenly had a prime suspect for the murder, and he was close enough that they could get there with an hour or so of driving. Maya looked over to Marco, and she could tell from the look on his face that he was thinking the same as she was.

"We need to get to Shreveport," Maya said. "Now."

CHAPTER EIGHTEEN

As they drove northwest towards Shreveport, taking Maya's rental car, Maya could feel her anticipation building. They'd found a suspect who seemed much more plausible to her than J.D. ever had, who had a connection to four murder victims, and who was just a couple of hours' drive away. It was a combination that might mean they could end all this today, well ahead of the deadline.

Even so, Maya was determined to be thorough. She wasn't going to make the same mistake that Sheriff Recks and his deputies had. She was going to make *sure* she had the killer before she declared all of this finished.

It was getting into the start of evening as they drove up along the highway, passing by the bayou, through parts of the state that were far more like the Louisiana of Maya's imagination, with open wetland spreading out on either side. Maya saw small boats out on it all, and passed many more towns as small as Pollock. They even passed by a sign promising a state alligator sanctuary.

Finally, Shreveport came into view, with its skyscrapers seeming almost to stick up out of the surrounding bayou. It hugged the banks of the Red River that the highway had been running alongside for most of the way there, lending a slightly different feel to it than Alexandria. It seemed more open somehow, less closed in by the spaces around it.

They weren't there to sightsee, though.

"What do we do if the address for Augustine Harmer isn't current?" Marco asked.

"Then we find him through the DMV, or we just ask at his place to find out if he left a forwarding address."

Maya was used to tracking down people who weren't there anymore. With cold cases, people moved on and got new lives. Sometimes, finding them could be the difference between solving a case or not. Marco presumably didn't have that problem, when he was used to dealing with fresh homicides.

"Honestly, though, I think this address will be good. He'd have to notify his probation officer of any change of address."

He would be there. There was no reason for him to think that anyone would be onto him. There was no reason for him to move.

"Do you think he gets put in prison deliberately?" Maya asked Marco as she drove. "He keeps getting put away, but for minor things, nothing that will see him locked away for life. Do you think he commits the crimes to get put away and look for his next victim?"

"Why bother?" Marco asked. "If he just wants to find a target, then he could find female corrections officers another way."

"Maybe it's just the way he knows," Maya suggested. "Or maybe he wants to see them in person before he kills them. Maybe it's just ritual at this point."

"Or maybe he does the small scale stuff compulsively, gets locked up, and only then starts to fixate on a guard. We don't have any way of knowing."

Maya had to admit that Marco had a point. "We'll just have to ask him when we get there."

They drove into Shreveport, which seemed to be geared much more towards tourists than Alexandria. Maya actually thought that she saw a group of them being led around by a guide, taking in the oldest of the city's buildings.

Maya was still taking it all in when she saw the police car pull out behind them, following close behind.

She sighed.

"Not again."

Sure enough, the lights came on, and a quick burst of the siren told her that she should pull over. She slid the Toyota over to the side of the road, turned the engine off, and waited.

"This doesn't make sense," she said. "We're in Shreveport. Sherriff Recks doesn't have any authority here."

"Sheriff Recks?"

"Pollock Sheriff's Department. The ones who put Johnathan Dennis in jail. They really don't like me now I've gotten him out."

"We'll sort all this out," Marco assured her. "We just need to stay calm."

He'd obviously seen the way Maya was starting to tense up at being harassed like this again. She'd played nice last time, but at some point, she was going to have to act, or she would never be able to finish her case.

Her mood only got worse when two cops, a man and a woman, got out of the car, with their hands going to their guns. Maya had to force herself to keep her hands where they would be able to see them. She lowered the window when the male cop gestured for her to do so.

"Is this your car?" the cop asked.

"It's a rental car," Maya replied.

"Step out of the vehicle please, both of you."

The cop was being polite about it, but Maya really didn't need this today.

"Listen-"

"Step out of the car, ma'am."

The male cop hadn't drawn his weapon, but the female cop with him had, as if already getting ready for the situation to escalate out of hand. Maya knew why: practically every training program for beat cops started with the horror stories, the ways things could get out of hand in just seconds. They tried to persuade them that if they weren't constantly on guard, this could be the time when a suspect came out shooting.

It just made the situation more dangerous.

With a sigh, Maya stepped out of the car, and saw Marco do the same.

"I'm Agent Maya Grey, with the FBI," she said. "My ID is in my jacket pocket. Can I reach for it?"

"Slowly," the male cop said.

Maya moved as slowly as she could, not wanting to risk spooking the cop who had a gun on her.

"Here, this is me. That's Detective Marco Spinelli of the Cleveland PD. He's consulting with me on a case."

"Consulting," the female cop said. "Why is a Cleveland cop consulting in Shreveport?"

"I worked with Maya on another case, linked to her current one," Marco said. He offered the cop a smile. "I like to help out."

He was turning up the charm, and maybe it was having some kind of effect, because the cop's expression softened a little. Her gun didn't lower, though.

"Officer," Maya said. "You're currently pointing your weapon at a federal agent."

The other woman seemed to realize what she was doing then and holstered her weapon. That was a start. Maya still wanted to know more, though.

"What's all this about?"

"We've had a report of this vehicle being stolen," the male cop said. "Our system flags the numberplates of stolen vehicles automatically."

A report that it was stolen. Maya could guess exactly where that had come from. Sheriff Recks was trying to waste her time. He was still trying to make her life difficult, trying to get his own petty revenge for Maya making him look bad. In other circumstances, it might have been a nuisance, but with a life on the line, maybe even her sister's, Maya didn't have the time to waste.

"Look," she said, "you can see that this is clearly not a stolen car, so can we get on our way? I'm in the middle of a murder investigation."

The male cop shook his head. "Sorry, but the vehicle *is* listed as stolen. That means we have to sort all of this out before we can let you go. I want you to come down to the station with us. We'll be able to establish exactly what's going on there."

Maya was starting to lose patience now. "I just told you that I'm an FBI agent in the middle of something more important."

"Or you could just be a con artist with a fake badge," the female cop said.

"Come on," Marco said. "How likely is that? This is some local sheriff trying to cause trouble, and we're talking about a murder here."

"Currently, we're talking about a stolen vehicle," the male cop said, in a tone that was apologetic, but firm. "Look, you have a choice. You can come with us to the station voluntarily to sort all of this out, or we can arrest you right now."

That wasn't much of a choice. If this had been one of the sheriff's deputies again, Maya might actually have lost her temper and taken them down. She didn't this time partly because there were two cops, one of whom was already trigger happy, and partly because they were clearly trying to do their jobs. Maya could even see their point: if someone just *claimed* to be FBI and flashed a badge to try to get out of being arrested, she would want to know far more.

"All right. We'll do it. We'll come to your station with you."

100

*

Everything took too much *time* for Maya. They took her and Marco to the station, sat them in an interview room, and took their IDs away to check them. After that, it was just a question of sitting there, waiting for the police to make the calls they needed to make to their bosses, to the car rental company, and to anyone else they wanted to check with.

Maya paced the room impatiently, knowing that every second she spent in here was time wasted she could be using to try to catch a murderer.

"There's nothing you can do to make it go faster, Grey," Marco said. He was sitting at the interview table, looking far more patient than Maya felt.

"That doesn't make this any less annoying. Sheriff Recks has gone too far with all this."

"So make a complaint about him."

"To whom?" Maya asked. "He's an elected sheriff, remember."

It meant doing anything about him almost impossible. Unless his behavior was so criminal that he could actually be arrested for it, then there was no real way to get rid of him, however much he was obstructing them in their case.

Eventually, finally, a detective came into the room, a man of about forty, in a sharp suit, open in a way that revealed the straps of his shoulder holster.

"Detective Stevens," he said, introducing himself. "Tell me, Agent, Detective, what are you doing in Shreveport?"

"Trying to track down a murderer," Maya said. "One we believe currently resides here. I take it you made the calls to confirm who we are, and that our car isn't stolen?"

"We did," Detective Stevens said. "Although when we called Cleveland PD, they had no idea that one of their detectives was down here."

"I'm using some of my vacation time to help with this," Marco said. "Is that going to be a problem, Detective?"

Detective Stevens shrugged. "Not for me. It's between you and your bosses. As for the rest of it, it seems that the whole thing was one big mistake. The wrong number plate put into the system, that's all."

"That's all?" Maya said. She didn't believe it for a minute. "That number plate was put in there deliberately by Pollock's Sheriff's

101

Department, in an effort to obstruct my investigation. Probably he thought he'd get really lucky and one of his deputies would be the first to see me."

Maya realized how badly that could have gone, because the sheriff wouldn't have acted anywhere near as quickly to resolve things. She might have found herself sitting in a cell for days.

"I think your superiors are going to make a call," Detective Stevens said. "But without any proof that this was done maliciously, we have to treat it as if it was all just a clerical error at their end. I suggest you do the same."

Sweep it under the rug. Don't react. Let the sheriff keep doing what he was doing. Maya didn't want to do any of that, but right then, she didn't have the time to do anything else.

She still had a murderer to catch.

"Are we free to go?" she asked.

"Yes. Technically, you were never under arrest, so you're welcome to go anytime you want." Detective Stevens held out the keys to Maya's rental car for her to take.

She snatched them from his grip and started for the door. Augustine Harmer was still there, waiting to be brought in, and Maya didn't have as much time to do it anymore.

CHAPTER NINETEEN

It was getting into evening by the time they pulled up outside Augustine Harmer's address. There were people out on the streets now, in some kind of festival that had crowds heading slowly down towards the river, some wearing t-shirts advertising a "grand shrimp boil," whatever that was.

The best thing about a rental car was that they could case Augustine Harmer's apartment block without it being obvious that they were cops. It was a run-down block, four stories high, in brownstone that had been badly whitewashed at the lowest levels. Between that and the weathering from the sun, it gave Maya the impression of a bald head sticking up through receding hair.

Maya stood outside, apparently checking her phone like a lost tourist, but actually carefully looking over the area for lines of escape. It was better to know which way someone might run *before* going to accuse them of being a serial killer.

Marco seemed to be giving the place the same professional once over.

"There will be a fire escape down to that alley at the rear. From there, it looks like a pretty straight shot down to the river."

"I'm pretty confident we could run him down before that," Maya said. "But if you want to stay and watch the rear of the building…"

"And leave you going in alone against a suspected serial killer?" Marco shook his head. "No way."

Maya thought about insisting. She wasn't sure that she wanted to put anyone else in danger, even a toughened cop like Marco. There was a reason that she liked working alone. At the same time, though, it was good to have backup in case this turned ugly and, besides, Maya doubted that she would be able to persuade Marco to just wait patiently outside.

That meant the two of them were going in together. Maya kept looking at the building for a few moments longer, making sure that there weren't any other escape routes, then started forward towards the entrance.

The first stage was to get into the building. Maya could have buzzed up to another resident to ask for entry, and she would if this took too long, but she preferred not to take the risk that they might be a friend of Augustine's who might warn him that the police were coming for him. It was better to be patient. That meant the two of them waiting in the doorway, trying not to look too conspicuous until someone came out. In this case, it was an older woman, wheeling a basket for whatever shopping she was going out to do.

Maya showed the woman her badge, holding it out at eye level and giving her plenty of time to check that it was real. "FBI, ma'am, we need to get inside."

"What's all this about?" the woman replied. She looked Maya up and down as though she couldn't quite believe even now that Maya could actually be an FBI agent.

"Does Augustine Harmer live here? Do you know if he's in?" Marco asked. It was good thinking. There would be nothing more embarrassing than showing up to arrest someone only to find that they were out. This wasn't like a package, where you left a little card so someone could rebook the time of their arrest.

"That no good lay-about? Of course he's here, playing his music through the walls, keeping me up to all hours. You here to arrest him for all the druggies he brings around this place?"

"Something like that," Maya said, although that was useful information. It meant that they potentially had something concrete they could hold him on while they got the physical proof they needed to tie him to the murders. Whatever he was doing was going to be in violation of his parole.

The first thing that Maya did as they started to go inside was check the buzzers for the different apartments, making sure that they had the right number. She and Marco headed upstairs, stepping out onto the landing to his apartment. Maya could hear the pulse of loud metal coming from inside.

"Ready?" Maya asked, drawing her weapon. With a man like this, they couldn't afford to take chances.

Marco drew his own sidearm. "Ready."

Maya hammered on the door. "Augustine Harmer, this is the FBI! Open up!"

There was no answer from inside. It was possible that he hadn't heard, given the volume of the music coming from inside.

104

"Let me try," Marco said. He moved forward to slam his fist against the door with his greater size and strength.

Some instinct flared in Maya, and she found herself pushing Marco to the side without even quite knowing why.

She heard the bark of a shotgun a moment later, and half the door disappeared.

Maya threw herself across the line of the door, trying to get a glimpse of where Harmer was in his apartment. She saw a couch that had been kicked over, saw a large, bulky man standing behind it with a shotgun in his hands. Maya got to the far side of the doorway as another shot came, missing her barely.

"Put the weapon down, Augustine!" she called out.

Another shot slammed into the wall, just a few hands from her head. The thin plasterwork of the walls wasn't going to be enough to stop the flying shot.

Marco fired back, leaning around the doorway and squeezing off shots before ducking his head back as the shotgun roared again. It was good to see him doing that, because it meant Maya knew for sure that he wasn't going to freeze up in a firefight.

Maya went into the doorway next, pushing forward, firing as she went more to ensure that Augustine wasn't going to have a chance to shoot her than to really take him down. Her eyes flicked round for traps or additional assailants. She saw a dark, dingy apartment with the curtains half drawn even in the day, with drug paraphernalia laid out on a table, and a whole selection of guns set out ready for the taking along one wall.

The one Augustine had in his hands was the only one Maya cared about right then, though. He ducked back down behind his couch, scuttled back, and went for the fire escape, abandoning his shotgun as he went. Maya set off in pursuit, not wanting to give him any respite.

He got through and set off down, with Maya and Marco in pursuit. Running like that, he presented an easy target, but he'd dropped the shotgun and wasn't firing back at them. Maya couldn't justify shooting him like that. Besides, she wanted him alive. She wanted to hear his confession for what he'd done. She wanted the absolute proof that would see another woman safe.

So Maya kept chasing, down the fire escape to ground level. Augustine was heading for the river now. *Did* he have a boat there?

Maya knew that she couldn't let him get away, and sprinted all the harder in his wake.

For a big man, Augustine Harmer was good at running. Maybe he'd been a football player once. More likely, he just knew that he needed to be able to run from the cops when they came. Had he been anticipating this moment since the first time he killed someone?

Did he have an escape route all planned out?

That was Maya's biggest fear. She and Marco had looked over the apartment complex, but there was no way of knowing what plans the fugitive in front of her might have put in place.

Currently, his plan seemed to be to lose them in the crowds of people heading down towards the river. The problem with that was that he was a large man, running through the crowds and pushing people out of the way as he went. It made tracking his progress easy, even as Maya slid around people, badge held high to try to get them to move.

"FBI, out of the way!"

A few of them moved, but more just turned to see what was happening, getting their phones out to record it all. No one moved to help catch Augustine.

Maya followed him down to the waterfront by the river, where there were marquees set up, and the smell of boiling seafood filled the air. There were even more people there, so that for a moment, Maya actually *did* lose sight of Augustine in the crowd.

One advantage of having Marco with her, though, was that he was more than tall enough to see over the rest of the people there.

"That way!" he called out, pointing to the spot where a jetty jutted out into the water, with numerous small boats moored around it.

Maya had been right; he was trying to get away over the water. For now, there was no time to think about how she might have done things differently, how she might have insisted that Marco watch the back or called in assistance from the local PD. For now, there was only the chase, trying to make sure that they got to Augustine Harmer before he could get away to kill again.

Maya raced through the crowd, dodging past a spot where people were barbequing. Ahead of her, she saw Augustine kick over another barbeque into her path, and Maya hurdled it, not slowing down as she sought to keep up the pressure on him.

They made it to the jetty, with him running for one of the boats there. It was small and sleek looking, probably fast enough to get out

106

into one of the bayous running off the main river and then lose itself completely.

Maya stopped, levelling her gun at Augustine, holding it steady, in spite of the sweat dripping from her brow, trying to keep focused on every movement he made.

"Augustine Harmer. Stop where you are."

He squared up to her, looking back at her defiantly as Marco caught up to Maya.

"You think I'm going back to prison again? I'm not going back there."

"Put your hands in the air, Augustine," Maya said. "Do it now. You're under arrest."

"I'm not going back," he replied. "You're going to have to kill me."

He was reaching down into the boat now, maybe to find the keys to get it started, maybe reaching for something else. Around Maya, she could see a crowd gathering, plenty with their phones out, recording the whole thing. If she got this wrong, probably even if she got it *right*, this would be all over the internet soon.

"I didn't come here to kill you, Augustine," Maya said. "Put your hands in the air where I can see them."

"Putting me back inside *is* killing me!" Augustine said.

He was actually trying to get her to shoot him. Maya had never had this happen to her, but she'd heard about it. She was caught in an impossible situation. If she put her gun away, he might come up with one of his own and start firing while she and Marco were out in the open with no cover. If she fired now, and there *wasn't* a gun there out of sight, she would have killed a man for no reason.

Maya compromised and lowered her weapon, without putting it away.

"You think that you don't have anywhere left to go, Augustine, but at least if you come with us, you have some hope. It's better than getting shot."

He was more likely to shoot if he thought there was no other way out. If he thought there was no chance of things turning out ok, then he had nothing to lose. Maya had to make him see that even prison was better than the alternative.

"Stupid bitch, you don't understand anything!"

His hand came up, and now Maya saw the gun in his hand, a big, silver .45 that he must have stashed on the boat for extra protection.

107

Maya's Glock came up even as he raised it, and in that moment, she found herself checking the space behind him for civilians, checking the lines of fire, all the things that she'd been trained to do both in the army and by the FBI.

She only had a split second, but that moment seemed to stretch out forever. In that moment, Maya had to choose. Did she take the shot? Did she put rounds into his center of mass until he went down? Or did she wait?

She found a third option, and fired.

Augustine cried out as the bullet hit him in the shoulder, dropping the weapon he held. He fell, staggering back into his boat, presumably because of the shock of it rather than the impact.

Maya was on him in an instant, putting her gun away even as she tossed his to Marco. She grabbed Augustine, dragging him onto his belly even while he cried out in pain. There were still cameras on her, but Maya was sure she'd done everything she could to stop this escalating before she'd fired.

"Augustine Harmer," Maya said. "You're under arrest."

CHAPTER TWENTY

Maya followed the ambulance to the hospital, not wanting to let Augustine Harmer out of her sight if she could help it.

It wasn't the kind of concern that she'd had for Liza Carty that made her go there for him. She just needed to make sure that he was going to live so that he could answer questions. The fact that he'd shot at them would be more than enough to get him sent back to jail, but that wasn't going to be enough for the kidnapper. Maya needed proof if she was going to make sure that he didn't kill one of his "bunnies" when the time until the deadline ran out.

The best way was to get a confession out of him.

For now, that meant pacing hospital corridors while Augustine went into surgery to have the damage her bullet had done repaired. Maya and Marco were stuck in a corridor outside the operating theatre, time seeming to pass by far too slowly.

Maya might have aimed to avoid the worst possible outcomes, but being hit by a bullet was still a big deal. She walked up and down outside the operating theater while Marco went to get them both coffee from a vending machine.

A nurse in scrubs came out of surgery after a while, obviously on her way to somewhere else. Maya stepped into her path.

"Is the surgery going ok? Will he live?"

"Are you a relative?" The nurse clearly knew that she wasn't.

"I'm an FBI agent who believes he has killed four women," Maya replied. "Will he live? When will I be able to question him?"

"He has lost a lot of blood," the nurse said. "Your bullet, I take it that it was yours, has nicked the brachial artery. We're working to repair it, but we anticipate him being out of surgery shortly. Why don't you go down to the waiting area downstairs, and someone will come fetch you when he's able to talk to you?"

Maya didn't want to wait, didn't want to feel yet more minutes dripping away from her deadline, yet it seemed that she didn't have much of a choice. Even as Marco came back out of the elevator holding coffee, Maya had to shake her head.

109

"They're making us wait downstairs. Come on."

"Are you sure?" He sounded a little worried. "Things downstairs are a bit… well, the local news is on."

Maya guessed that would mean a starring role for her, Marco, and Augustine, but she wasn't about to shy away from any of that. Shrugging, she stepped into the elevator.

The waiting area downstairs was busy, with plenty of injured or sick people waiting for the doctors to be able to get to them. The whole space was an institutional blue-gray, with a couple of potted plants and art prints not making it look any cheerier. Maya took a plastic seat in one corner, settling down to wait.

All the while, in the corner, it was impossible for Maya to take her eyes off the screen where it showed grainy phone footage of her taking Augustine down. The headline was "shooting at Shrimp Boil" as if Maya had just been some random shooter, and not an FBI agent stopping a very dangerous man before he could kill her and her…

…what was Marco at this point? Was he her partner? Her friend? Something else? That thought occupied several more seconds as Maya stared at the screen.

"You didn't do anything wrong," Marco said. "Frankly, I'm amazed you managed to keep from killing him. I was on the verge of pulling the trigger myself."

"If he dies, then we don't get a confession," Maya said. "We have evidence, but it's all circumstantial so far. It might convince a jury, but I want to be sure."

"So that means taking a riskier shot even though it might have meant him shooting *you*?" Marco said. "What, did you think I wouldn't see that?"

Maya had hoped that it wouldn't be obvious. Even so, she wasn't going to apologize for it now.

"I can't risk him dying if it might cost my sister her life," Maya said.

"And what about your life? Do you think that doesn't matter?"

"I think it's the risk I signed up for." Maya had known the risks she was taking when she joined the army and then the FBI. Megan hadn't signed up for those risks.

"You didn't sign up to have to hold back while someone else tries to shoot you," Marco said.

"I'll do whatever I have to do in order to keep her safe, Marco. Besides, it worked out ok, didn't it?"

"This time." Marco's look of worry didn't even begin to ease. Maya wished that she could make that look go away, but it wasn't as though she could pretend that she would give up on anything that would help her to complete her investigation and save another woman.

*

Maya was still contemplating exactly how far she would go when the nurse eventually came to fetch them.

"He's awake now," she said. "He'll be a little disoriented from the anesthetic, but he should be able to talk to you. I'll lead you to him."

Maya and Marco followed along in the nurse's wake, heading for what turned out to be a private room away from the hustle and bustle of the main wards. It seemed wrong to Maya that someone like Augustine Harmer should get that kind of privacy, but it also made sense, because who would want someone as dangerous as him around the other patients?

Maya let herself into the room, and was just in time, because she saw Augustine trying to get out of bed. He was weak enough that he more or less collapsed as he did it, but she and Marco were there to catch him. They hauled him back into bed, and Marco took out some handcuffs, cuffing one of his wrists to one of the rails of the bed.

"Going somewhere, Augustine?" Marco asked.

"Screw you, cop," Augustine snapped.

Maya just waited for his eyes to fall on her.

"You! You shot me!"

He said it as if Maya should have just stood there and let him shoot her instead.

"Because you shot at us," Maya pointed out. "You're going back to prison for that, Augustine. That, and the guns, and the drugs."

"I've never seen any of those things before in my life!"

It was an automatic denial, clearly without any hope of actually succeeding. Maya ignored that, cutting straight to the part of this that mattered.

"Why did you kill them, Augustine?"

That made Augustine freeze in the middle of his anger and his indignation. Maya saw the surprise there, the shock. Was that shock at

111

someone having worked out the connection between his killings, or was it something else?

"Kill someone?" Augustine said. "You think I killed someone?"

"I think you murdered four people. Samantha Neele, Kelly Brooker, Adawe Ali, and Justine Kells. I think you went into their homes and stabbed them. What was it, Augustine? Was it just that you hated prison guards?"

"I never killed anyone!" Augustine protested.

"Because you're such a stand-up guy?" Marco asked, from the other side of his bed. "Because you hesitated even for a second before firing a shotgun blind through a door at us?"

"Because I couldn't go back to jail!" Augustine wrenched at the handcuffs holding him. "But that was me defending myself! I've never sneaked into people's homes. I've never stabbed anyone, even a prison guard."

Defending himself. Probably in his head, that was exactly what he had been doing. The fact that it had involved trying to kill two people seemed to elude him.

"So you're saying that you had nothing to do with the murders?" Maia asked.

"Of course I'm saying that, and you can't prove any of this bullshit!"

"Except that we have a pretty important piece of evidence," Maya said. Maybe if she presented him with it, he would just come out and admit it. Maybe it would all be done with. "We looked at parole files, Augustine, to find who had been in the prisons that these four guards had worked in. We looked, and do you know how many people were at all those different prisons, at the same time that the guards worked there? Do you know how many of them were out at exactly the times that the murders took place?"

She could see the fear on Augustine's face.

"You're not pinning this on me."

"You're the only one who fits," Marco said. "A violent man, out at just the right time to kill four women."

"When?" Augustine demanded. "When were these murders?"

"The most recent one was eighteen months ago, in August," Maya said. "In Texas."

The moment she saw the relief on Augustine's face, she knew that something had gone badly wrong. Augustine actually laughed, and

112

Maya couldn't tell if he was laughing with relief or laughing at her and Marco.

"Then you've got nothing!" Augustine said. "Because I was nowhere near Texas that August. I was in Alaska! I joined a crab fishing crew. Didn't make the money I should have. Got screwed over on the whole job. But I can get you their number. I have an *alibi*."

Maya could feel her heart falling into her boots as her case unraveled. She felt numb. She'd put so much effort into this, and now Augustine had an alibi?

"I'm glad you feel so happy, Augustine," Marco said. "Maybe that satisfaction will help when you go back to jail."

"But I didn't kill anyone!"

"You still tried to shoot a federal agent," Maya said. "Your house is still full of drugs and guns. Goodbye, Augustine."

She walked out of the room with Marco, doing her best to hide her disappointment. She was halfway down the hall to the exit when she saw two people coming the other way that she *definitely* didn't want to talk to.

Sheriff Recks was there, walking alongside Detective Stevens.

"What are *you* doing here?" Maya asked Recks. "Did you drive all this way just to cause trouble?"

"I saw the little shootout on the news, and I wanted to be here when you caught the fallout from that," the sheriff said, not bothering to hide his dislike.

"I would have thought hiding away and fabricating an accusation of a stolen car would be more your style," Maya said. "Or maybe getting a man sent to prison for a crime he didn't commit."

"At least I didn't shoot anyone," Sheriff Recks snapped back.

"That's enough," Detective Stevens said. "I said you could come along because you more or less showed up at my door demanding it, and because my department has a policy of playing nice with the sheriff's departments of the state."

Somehow, he made that sound like an apology. Maya guessed that she wouldn't like the next part.

"Detective Spinelli," Detective Stevens asked. "What was your involvement in the events of today?"

"Because you've no business being here," Sheriff Recks said, with a nasty look.

113

Maya saw what game he was playing then. If he could say that Marco was acting illegally because he was outside his jurisdiction, then Marco might find himself arrested for his part in all this. Breaking and entering, brandishing a weapon, the works.

Maya had put up with enough.

"Detective Spinelli is here in Louisiana as a consultant on my case," Maya said. "I was the one who led the raid on Augustine Harmer's apartment, and I was the one who shot him. Do you have a problem with that, Sheriff Recks?"

"Well, I-"

"Because I have a problem with you," Maya said, taking a step towards him that made the bigger man back up. "From the moment I got here, you have harassed me and slowed me down. Now, you're here pushing bullshit allegations that have no legal basis. So I'm going to say this: if you get in my way even one more time, so much as slow me down for a minute, I'm going to be the one arresting *you*, for obstructing a murder investigation."

She saw the sheriff redden, and Detective Stevens got in the way. Maya had things she wanted to say to him, too.

"Detective Stevens, Augustine Harmer has turned out not to be the killer I'm looking for, but the moment you search his apartment, you will find more than enough evidence to send him straight back to jail. I'm all over the local news, so you can see for yourself that I was completely justified in taking the shot when I did. Now, I'm going to head back to Alexandria, staying very carefully under the speed limit at all times." She gave Sheriff Recks an angry look. "Frankly, I'm getting tired of this bullshit, and I still have a killer to catch."

114

CHAPTER TWENTY ONE

Maya headed back to Alexandria with Marco, feeling dejected. It was getting far too late now, partly thanks to the drive to Shreveport and back, partly because of all the time that Sheriff Recks had managed to waste for them.

"I hate that man," Maya declared as they got to their hotel. She was tired and angry, with a lot of that anger flowing the sheriff's way.

"Who? The receptionist? He's ok," Marco replied, with a grin that said he was trying to lighten the mood.

"You know who, Marco."

"The sheriff."

He'd made Maya lose her temper, and she hated losing her temper. It meant that she'd lost control. In a way, it meant that the other person had won. People talked about catharsis, but Maya preferred keeping things locked down, not letting the world affect her.

"He's... how can someone working in law enforcement be more interested in causing trouble for the FBI than in trying to solve a murder?"

"You know as well as I do that half of law enforcement is politics," Marco pointed out.

"Well, it shouldn't be."

Maya hated the fact that it was. She hated the time that she had to spend dealing with this stuff rather than hunting for a killer, trying to save her sister. Maybe Harris liked this side of things, but Maya simply didn't have the taste for it.

"It shouldn't be, but if things were as they should be, then there wouldn't be much of a need for cops."

They headed upstairs to their rooms.

"Come in for a little while?" Maya said. She realized how that had to sound. "I won't be able to sleep if we don't get *something* that can keep this case moving forward."

For a moment, she found herself thinking about the *other* reason for inviting someone into her room. It was hard not to with Marco there in front of her. He was that good looking.

115

"Sure," he said.

They went inside. Marco took the room's only chair, while Maya perched on the bed with her laptop. Ordinarily for something like this she would have grabbed coffee, but now she got out a miniature bottle of bourbon from the minibar. If Harris questioned the expenses, she would explain it as entirely necessary given the involvement of the local sheriff.

"Where did we go wrong, Marco?" That was the part that Maya couldn't understand. "Where was the flaw in my logic?"

"I'm not sure you did anything *wrong*," Marco said.

Maya knocked back the bourbon. The burn of it helped a little, but not enough. A part of her wanted to go back to the minibar, but she didn't. Maya needed to take the edge off, not lose control. She needed to be able to think, and she couldn't do that if she just kept drinking.

"I must have gotten something wrong, or we'd have solved this by now. Augustine Harmer would be our guy, and we'd be done."

Yet somehow, they weren't. Harmer wasn't going to walk free after everything else he'd done, but he wasn't the murderer they were looking for either.

Maya opened up her laptop, wanting to be sure that she hadn't missed something.

"I want to go over this again. I want to check whether there's someone else who meets all the criteria out there in the records."

"You know there isn't," Marco said. "You did all of this yourself the first time around."

"Well, maybe I got something wrong."

It was the only explanation. She'd messed up. She'd found a promising looking lead, but only because she'd missed something, or ignored something. Did that make Maya as bad at her job as Sheriff Recks?

Ordinarily that would have been a bad enough thought, but the wasted time was a worse one. Maya had used up a couple of days now, and she was no further along than when she'd started. Suddenly, a week was starting to look a lot less generous than it had when Maya had begun this investigation.

She ran through the process she'd been through again. First, establish the group of victims. That didn't seem to be in doubt. There were still four female prison officers who had been killed within a few years of one another, all in crimes that shared the same MO.

116

"We're definitely looking for a serial killer," Maya said. "That part isn't in doubt. Or at least, the odds on it being a coincidence are pretty... it *couldn't* just be a coincidence, could it, Marco?"

It was hard not to doubt even that with everything that had just happened.

"No," Marco replied. "Stop doubting yourself, Grey."

"It's difficult not to after the monumental way I just messed up."

"Following a lead that didn't pan out? We've all had those, and you know it. Think about all the blind alleys we had to go down with the last case, and you still found the killer."

"An hour too late," Maya pointed out. "I get the feeling that the kidnapper isn't going to be as generous about the deadline this time."

They couldn't afford to waste time. They had to get this *right*. Which meant going back through and finding the point in all this where she'd gone wrong last time.

She tried to focus. "All right, assume for a moment that the serial killer thing is solid. We looked through the probation records, cross referencing them with the times the guards worked at the different prisons. Is it possible that we got the dates wrong? That there could be someone else who overlapped with the four?"

Maya looked over the dates again, looking into the fragments of personnel files included in the case files for the four women. She tried looking through the old remains of their social media, but that didn't really get her any further. Three of the four hadn't mentioned their jobs, while the dates Samantha Neele gave matched up exactly with the ones that Maya already had.

She ran those dates through the probation files again, and slammed her laptop closed in frustration.

"It just gives me the same name: Augustine Harmer. It's no use."

Maya knew that she couldn't give up, but it was so hard not to when there just seemed to be a brick wall that she was slamming into, over and over again. She wanted to run the names of the people in prison again, but what did they say about the definition of insanity being doing the same thing again and again, expecting different results?

Maya tried to think of something else that she could do that might be useful.

"What else is there, Marco? Are there any other links between them beyond being prison guards? We need to find out more about these women."

117

She turned the laptop so that Marco could see, opened it up, and tried to find some link between the women beyond them being prison guards. Was there some other context in which someone might have met all four?

"What kind of connection are you looking for?" Marco asked.

Maya looked up at him, shaking her head. "I wish I knew. Maybe they all attended the same conferences related to their work? Maybe they all went to the same court at some point in order to collect a prisoner?"

Both of those sounded like long shots, even to her. Even so, Maya did her best to check them, but *how* was she meant to do something like that? She scoured the women's social media, working through whatever was still left, looking for any points of connection. When that failed, she started to go through the case files again.

It only fueled Maya's frustration. Maybe the bourbon was just making her mind work less efficiently, but no detail leapt out at her.

"Can *you* see anything?" Maya asked Marco.

"Nothing so far." He looked worried.

"Which brings us back to the prisons, and their prisoners, and-"

"Maya, you're going around in circles."

Now Maya realized that the worry wasn't about the case, it was about her.

"I need to keep going over it until I find something that-"

Marco was already shaking his head, though. "You need to stop, at least for tonight. Look at things with fresh eyes tomorrow."

"I can't afford to stop," Maya said. "My sister-"

"Isn't going to be saved tonight."

Maya realized that he was being deliberately reasonable with her, and it was only then that she realized that she was starting to panic. She'd been through a firefight and it hadn't touched her, but *this* was making her heart pound against the walls of her chest, and her breath come short.

Or had the firefight had some effect? Only a psychopath shot someone and didn't feel anything. It was just that sometimes, it took a while for those feelings to filter through, time to realize that things weren't ok.

Maya wasn't ok by then at all. Maybe that was why she'd reacted so badly to the sheriff before. Maybe that why she still had the urge to head over to the minibar and keep drinking. Maybe that was why she

118

wanted to pick a fight with Marco right now for saying something like that.

"She's my sister, Marco. You think I'm just going to give up?"

To Maya's surprise, Marco took her by the arms, physically lifting her away from the computer. Maya got ready to snap at him again.

"I'm not asking you to give up, I'm saying that you should get some rest. Come at this again tomorrow, when you've got a clearer head. When you've got some distance between yourself and what happened today."

Had he seen through her so easily?

It was almost as if that burst the bubble of Maya's tension. In that moment, she could breathe again, although her heart was still beating rapidly. It took her a moment or two to realize that had a lot to do with just how close Marco was to her now.

They were *very* close. Close enough that Maya could smell the musk of his aftershave. Close enough that Maya found herself wondering about what those muscles of his might feel like under her fingers, and about just how his lips would taste. For all that he was tall and strong, she had the suspicion that he would be a soft, delicate kisser.

All she would have to do in order to find out was move forward, just a little. Maya actually started to lean forward.

She was quite surprised when Marco took a step back.

"I'm sorry," Maya said, suddenly embarrassed. What had she been thinking, assuming that there was any chance that Marco would want to go that far with her when they'd only met one another... what? A couple of weeks back now?

"It's not anything you've done," Marco said.

"You just don't feel the same way?"

"You're asking me if I find you attractive?" Marco asked. "Of course I do, and if the situation were different, then maybe something would happen. When I thought it was just going to be Cleveland, I even *wanted* something to happen."

"But?" Maya said, because clearly *something* was holding him back.

"But this isn't just the work equivalent of a holiday romance anymore," Marco said. "If I'm going to be around, if we're going to keep working together on this, then we can't afford to complicate it with a relationship. You understand, don't you, Maya?"

119

Maya understood, but that didn't make it any less difficult. It didn't make the sense of something lingering between her and Marco go away and didn't take away the urge to kiss him anyway. He was right, though. They shouldn't do this when they were basically colleagues now.

Colleagues. For some reason, that word stuck in Maya's mind. It took her several seconds for her to realize the reason why.

"Colleagues," she said.

"What?"

"We've been looking at this wrong. I focused on the prisoners who were in the places these women worked, but they weren't the only ones there. All of them had colleagues, other prison guards, prison chaplains, wardens, doctors. How many of those will work at multiple prisons?"

It was far more likely than one prisoner being in all those separate places. It gave them somewhere else to look, and maybe, just maybe, they might be able to find an answer.

CHAPTER TWENTY TWO

The most frustrating part for Maya was having to wait until the next morning before she could work on the case more. Marco had made sure of that by putting her laptop under his arm when he left, ignoring Maya's protests.

"You need the sleep," he said.

That left Maya with a restless night, sleeping only because she was so tired after the investigations of the day before. She found herself dreaming of what might have happened if Marco hadn't pulled away at the last moment. She found herself imagining the muscles there under his shirt, glimpses of him coming out of any kind of order, building in intensity.

Then, pulling away almost as quickly as Marco had the previous evening, the dream faded, leaving Maya to wake blinking in the morning light. She showered and dressed as quickly as she could, then went over to hammer on Marco's door. She'd done what he wanted and gotten some sleep. Now he couldn't keep her from pursuing the angle she'd thought of last night.

There was no answer from his room, but when Maya went downstairs, she found him waiting at the breakfast table with other guests already eating elsewhere in the dining room. He'd obviously picked out food for both of them, because there were sausages, fresh orange juice and muesli set out there for her. Maya's laptop was in the middle of it all.

"Food first?" Marco suggested.

Maya shook her head. "I can multi-task."

She started to eat while she started up her laptop and tried to start the search for someone who had worked with all four of the dead prison guards. That meant finding personnel files for four prisons, but the advantage she had there was that they'd all been federal prisons.

Maya made a request via email, labeled it urgent, and sent a text to Harris to reinforce it. She started to eat, and almost before she had finished, her email pinged with a reply.

That reply held the personnel files she needed. Maya sent them over to Marco, who started to look through them on his phone.

"Look for names that repeat," she said. "We're looking for anyone who was at all four at the same time as the women who died."

While Marco started to look through the files, Maya started to set up a search. She used the names of the victims and the date range to cut away anyone who hadn't worked with any of them. That still left plenty of guards and other workers on the lists.

Now, it was a question of finding names that repeated.

There was no better way to do that than to scan through them, taking each name and searching for it in the other files. Maya worked through them, and little by little she started to cross off names. It was easier to find who *couldn't* be the killer, than who could.

Then one name snagged at her attention, one name that she knew, that she'd heard before. Jeremiah Wood. It took her a moment or two to realize exactly where she'd heard that name before.

That was the name of one of the corrections officers from the prison. The one who had met Maya at the reception of the place. The head guard there.

"I've found something," she said. "Someone who worked at all four. But I want to look him up a little more before we go rushing after him."

"Who?"

"His name's Jeremiah Wood but keep looking. There might be others."

It seemed more likely than with the prisoners. Maya didn't want to run after one corrections officer if the real killer was there watching, and used the opportunity to escape. After she'd gone after Augustine Harmer in such a rush, she wanted to be certain this time.

So she looked through Jeremiah Wood's personnel files, through his social media, through everything else she could find that might give herself an insight into the man.

Maya saw the way he'd gotten the top job at the prison, just months after Samantha Neele's death opened it up. She the likes and retweets for posters who clearly hated women. She saw one warning on his file for harassing a female colleague. The more she read, the more certain she was that she'd gotten the right man.

"Is there anyone else it could be?" Maya asked Marco.

"There's no one else on all four lists," he said. "I'm sure of it."

Which meant that they'd found a new prime suspect for Samantha's murder. It was time for them to head back to the prison to have a conversation with Jeremiah Wood.

*

Maya kept a careful eye out for the sheriff's deputies as she drove herself and Marco back to the prison. The last thing she wanted right then was yet another confrontation as the sheriff tried to stop her from doing her job. She drove within the speed limit, but it was hard to do it when she felt so sure that she was heading towards someone who was a good candidate to be Samantha Neele's killer.

Then again, that had been exactly how she'd felt with Augustine.

Maya was determined to take her time with this, to make sure that she did it right. It didn't matter that, in her mind, he was an obvious candidate. It didn't matter that he'd been stand-offish and arrogant when she'd visited the prison before, or that he obviously didn't like her looking into the case. What mattered was getting the proof she needed to tie him to the death.

At least she was pretty sure that he hadn't been working out of state at the time of the murder, this time.

"How are you going to play this?" Marco asked her.

"Don't worry, I'm going to play this cool," Maya assured him.

"Actually, I was about to suggest the opposite. When we met Jeremiah in the breakroom before, it was pretty obvious that he didn't like you. If he has a problem with women, maybe you can use that."

Maya smiled at that thought. "You're not just a pretty face, Detective Spinelli."

Too late, Maya realized what she'd just said.

"About that," Marco said, as they made their way up the long, winding road that led towards the prison. "About last night. I hope you know that it wasn't some kind of slight on you. It's just… I'm serious about doing this work, and I don't think we can work together if there's anything between us. We'd spend all our time trying to keep one another out of danger rather than doing our jobs."

He had a point, but that didn't make it any easier to bear. Maya had been on the verge of doing far more than kissing him last night.

"I already pulled you out of the way of a shotgun blast. It must be love," Maya joked.

123

"I never thanked you for that, did I?"

Maya shrugged. "If you have to thank your partner for things like that, then they aren't really your partner."

Marco gave her a serious look. "And *am* I your partner?"

That question caught Maya a little off guard. In every technical sense, of course, the answer was no. Marco wasn't even FBI, and Maya had always resisted every attempt by her boss to make her have a partner. Yet Marco was there with her on the case, there to bounce ideas off of or to have her back in dangerous situations. He'd come out here without even being asked, just because she needed him.

"I guess you are," Maya said, surprised by that even as she said it.

"You guess?" Marco sounded faintly amused by it. He could obviously see Maya's discomfort at the thought of having a partner.

"Maybe, possibly. If you're lucky."

It was hard to remember that they shouldn't be flirting, that Marco had a point about relationships with people he worked with. Maya distracted herself by concentrating on the road.

They made it to the prison and went inside. Yet another guard was on reception duty. Maya handed over her ID for him to check.

"I'm Agent Grey with the FBI, this is Detective Spinelli, my partner." She added that part for Marco's amusement. "We need to talk to Jeremiah Wood. It's urgent."

"I think he's patrolling the yard at the moment," the guard said. "You can wait for him in the break room, if you like."

Maya thought about demanding that he be pulled away from his work, but she knew enough about how prisons work to know that might leave a blind spot in which someone might get hurt. She could wait, just a little longer.

Even so, it was frustrating, sitting there in the break room, watching guards come and go, waiting for the moment when Jeremiah Wood finally stepped into the place, sauntering in and more or less ignoring Maya as he went to get coffee. He finally looked over at Maya with obvious contempt, and she found herself wondering if that was the way he'd looked at Samantha Neele and the others. Had that been a part of it? Had he just not been able to stand women working in the same job, or worse, in positions superior to his own?

"What are *you* doing back again?" he demanded as he started to drink his coffee.

"Trying to find a killer," Maya said.

She saw Marco move over to the entrance to the room. It didn't look like much, but it would stop Jeremiah from running, if he chose to.

"You *had* a killer, but no, you had to find a way to let him go. Is that how you do things in the FBI?"

"Letting innocent people go?" Maya retorted. "We try to. Right now, I'm trying to find the real killer. I thought maybe you could help me with that."

Jeremiah snorted at that. "What, you want me to do your job for you? Always the same with women like you. Sooner or later, you need a man to do the difficult parts of the job, and then you take the glory."

"Is that what it was like with Samantha Neele?" Maya asked. "You were the one doing all the work, and she got the top job?"

Jeremiah gave her another look of contempt and moved over to one of the chairs there, sitting down. "What do you think?"

"I *think* you were working at four prisons at the same time that female prison guards died, all killed in the same way. I think you're the only point of connection between those prisons, aside from one inmate who has an alibi. Tell me, Jeremiah, did you *notice* that four guards you worked with died the same way? Did you mention it to anyone?"

"My guess is he didn't," Marco said from the doorway. "Because he wouldn't want to incriminate himself."

"Was that it?" Maya asked. "Were you just trying to avoid suspicion?"

"This is bullshit," Jeremiah said. "I don't have to sit here and listen to this."

Maya shrugged. "You're right. This would be a lot better down at the local police station. Why don't we go there?"

"I'm not going anywhere with you," Jeremiah said.

"I'm going to have to insist," Maya said.

Jeremiah stood, looking over towards Marco. "What are you going to do? Have your boyfriend there try to arrest me. I've taken down bigger guys than him, plenty of times."

"Oh, I'm not going to ask Marco to do anything," Maya said, stepping forward.

Jeremiah's features seemed caught between contempt and amusement as she stepped in close to him. He grabbed for her, but Maya had anticipated that move. Big guys always liked to grab, always liked to throw their weight around. She twisted into the grab, hooking her leg behind Jeremiah's and sending him tumbling to the floor.

He came up, reaching for the nightstick at his belt. He swung it at Maya, and she ducked, then dodged aside from a second sweep of it. As a third swept by her head, Maya stepped in and threw a right cross, timing it to meet Jeremiah's jaw just as his weight was coming forward. He staggered and went down. He struggled to get up, still flailing with the nightstick. Maya grabbed his arm, wrenching it hard enough that he had a simple choice between letting go of the weapon or breaking his own arm. As it clattered to the break room floor, she pulled his arms behind his back and cuffed him.

"Jeremiah Wood, you're under arrest."

CHAPTER TWENTY THREE

Because it was the closest station, Maya had to drive Jeremiah out to the sheriff's office in Pollock. However much she disliked the man, it was the correct place to conduct the next part of this.

She left Marco behind, partly because it avoided any more accusations from Sheriff Recks about Marco overstepping his bounds and partly because it meant that Marco could stay behind at the prison, asking the other staff there about Jeremiah. It felt strange to leave that kind of thing to someone else, strange not to have control of the process, but Maya trusted Marco to do it.

That was part of what having a partner was about.

"Bitch, I'll have your badge for this!" Jeremiah snarled from the back seat of the Toyota.

"You have the right to remain silent, Jeremiah," Maya replied. "Why don't you use it for a while?"

Driving a suspect alone in a rental car like this wasn't ideal. It put Jeremiah behind her, and even though his hands were cuffed, there was still the danger that he might try something on the drive over to the sheriff's station. He certainly seemed agitated enough, and Maya found herself keeping half an eye on him throughout the journey.

It made watching the road more difficult, but thankfully, out here, there was nothing coming the other way. When Pollock showed up ahead, she headed straight to the sheriff's station, and pulled up outside. She dragged Jeremiah out of the car and forced him towards the station.

Sheriff Recks actually met them at the door. He must have seen them out of the windows to his office. One look at his reddening face told Maya that she needed to brace herself for a confrontation.

"What are you doing?" he demanded.

"Bringing in a suspect I've just arrested," Maya replied. "You're the nearest station, so this is where I'm bringing him."

"You've arrested Jeremiah?"

Maya noted the use of the guard's first name.

"You two know one another?" Maya said.

127

"We drink in the same bar," Sheriff Recks said. Somehow, Maya wasn't surprised. "And that's why I know that Jeremiah couldn't have done any of this! This is ludicrous!"

"He's a suspect I have good evidence to arrest. You do know what one of those is, Sheriff?" Maya couldn't resist the last part of it. She'd put up with so much from the sheriff in the last few days, and all of this was because he hadn't been bothered to do his job properly in the first place.

"This is nonsense!" Sheriff Recks said.

He was in between Maya and the door, but Maya pushed past him, shoving Jeremiah ahead of her. The same deputy as usual was there at the reception desk, looking almost as unhappy as the sheriff was about Maya's presence there.

"Which way are your interrogation rooms?" Maya demanded, putting enough authority into her voice that the deputy pointed even before he had a chance to think about it.

"Is the sheriff ok with this?" he asked, too late.

Maya was already marching Jeremiah through to the interrogation room, which was just a small, white painted room with a table and a couple of chairs, a camera looking down from the corner and a digital recorder on the table.

"Do you want a lawyer present?" Maya asked, as she turned the recorder on. She wasn't going to let the prison guard get away with this on a technicality.

"A lawyer? You think I'm paying some shyster to deal with this nonsense?"

"There's nothing nonsensical about murder," Maya said. "You can't just brush this aside."

"Why not?" Jeremiah demanded. "What do you think you have... Agent?"

He paused just long enough before he said that last word to show his contempt.

"I think that you're the only man who worked at four prisons at the same time as female prison guards who were murdered in their homes. I think you benefited directly from Samantha Neele's death. I think you hate women who work in tough jobs, and you particularly hate it when they tell you what to do. Do you want to tell me that I've gotten any of this wrong, Mr. Wood?"

He grunted.

128

"Please say it, for the benefit of the recording," Maya said. "Did you work at the same prisons as Samantha Neele, Kelly Brooker, Adawe Ali, and Justine Kells?"

"Yes, obviously," Jeremiah said. "Are you going to ask me stupid questions all day, or can we get to the part where I have your badge for this?"

"If you want to make a complaint to my boss at the FBI, I'm sure he'll consider it," Maya replied. "But in the meantime, we'll keep going with the questioning. Did you know the four women I just named?"

"Of course I did," Jeremiah said. He looked bored with this, if anything, as if expecting the whole thing to come to an end soon and for things to be fine for him. Was he really expecting his friend the sheriff to get him out of a murder charge?

"Then you'll also remember when each of them was murdered," Maya said. "You should, because you were working at the same prison as each of them when they were killed."

"So you think it was me?" Jeremiah snapped back. "Do you have any proof?"

"Do *you* have an alibi?"

After so long, physical proof was going to be hard to find, but if Maya could show that the rest of the evidence around Jeremiah was strong enough, then she didn't *need* to get fingerprints for him from one of the scenes, or find a knife with the victims' DNA on it in his possession.

"An alibi?"

"For just *one* of the killings," Maya said. "You can presumably remember when they all were pretty well. I know *I* would remember if someone I worked with were murdered. But I suppose these were just women, weren't they? They didn't really matter to you."

"How am I meant to remember exactly where I was years ago?"

"You don't remember where you were the night Samantha Neele died?"

Maya wasn't sure that she believed that. Did Jeremiah really care so little about any of his coworkers that he couldn't remember anything about the time when they'd died?

"All right, let's try something simpler. What was your relationship like with Samantha Neele?"

"We were co-workers. What do you want me to say?"

129

"I want the truth," Maya said. "You didn't like her, did you Jeremiah?"

"I... no, I didn't. She was as pushy and self-righteous as you are, Agent."

"Is *that* why you killed her? Is that why you killed three other guards?"

"I didn't do any of that!"

From his reaction, though, Maya could tell that he was hiding something. It was just a question of what. Maya was about to press him further when Sheriff Recks burst into the interview room.

"That's enough!" he said. "You can't go around accusing good, upstanding members of the community of things like this!"

"For the benefit of the recording, Sheriff Recks of the Pollock Sheriff's Department has just entered the interview room. Uninvited."

That only seemed to fuel the sheriff's anger. "I don't need to be invited. This is my station. Now, release that man!"

"Not when he's my most promising suspect for the murder of Samantha Neele, no."

"Agent, I'm telling you to let Jeremiah go right now. You've made a mistake bringing him in."

Maya wasn't going to back down as easily as that. She stood and faced the sheriff. "This is an FBI investigation. It has nothing to do with you, sheriff. It's certainly not your decision who I do and don't release."

"You just made a big mistake," the sheriff said. "Jeremiah Wood is a good man, a pillar of this community. I've known him for years, and there's no way that he could ever kill someone."

"Given that a man has just been in prison for years based on your assessment of what he was capable of, you'll forgive me if I don't let him go based on your word."

The sheriff stepped forward, and for a moment Maya thought that he might make some kind of grab at her. She half hoped that he would, because then she would have all the justification she needed to take him down.

"This is my county, and my station. You'll let him go, or I swear I'll arrest you. I'll see you sued for every cent you're worth for wrongful arrest!"

Maya's sister was currently missing, caught in the clutches of a kidnapper. Compared to that, did the sheriff really believe that his threats meant anything?

"If you want to try to arrest me, do it," Maya said. "But the moment you do so, the detective working with me will make a call to my boss, and you'll have FBI agents crawling over your station, looking into everything you've ever done. This is my prisoner, and my arrest."

Her phone rang then, and Maya saw that it was Marco.

"I'm going outside to take this," she said. "I expect my prisoner to still be here when I get back."

She walked outside and answered the call.

"How are things going over there?" Marco asked her.

"The sheriff is being his usual cooperative self. Making threats, insisting that it can't be Jeremiah because they're drinking buddies."

"From where I'm standing, that only makes it more likely that he's guilty."

Maya refrained from commenting. She didn't like the sheriff any more than Marco did, but it didn't change anything about the case. She was hoping, though, that Marco might have something that would.

"Has he talked, yet?" Marco asked.

"He's still treating the whole thing like it's a joke," Maya said. "But he couldn't provide an alibi for any of the murders. Do you have anything at your end?"

She wished that she could have been there for the interviews with the other staff at the prison, but she'd needed to bring Jeremiah in. She'd needed to book him, to do this properly.

"Plenty," Marco said. "It seems that people are a lot more willing to talk when he's not around. Especially after they heard that he's been taken down. Suddenly, they're not so afraid to say what they really think about him."

Which meant that they'd been afraid before.

"So he's a bully?" Maya asked. It fit with what she'd seen of Jeremiah.

"With both the staff and the prisoners. The kind of guy you really don't want in any kind of position of power in a prison."

And he'd made it to be head guard. He'd gotten into a position to do whatever he wanted.

"What kinds of things did the other guards say?" Maya asked.

"That he's not above using violence with prisoners, then passing it off as dealing with a threat. That he hates the idea of taking orders from anyone, especially if it's a woman. That he's harassed female guards in the past, and gotten angry if they've tried to call him out on it."

No doubt if they went back through the rest of the places Jeremiah had worked, they would find a similar story. With a man like that, everyone stayed quiet until one person opened the floodgates. Then it all came rushing out.

"Then there's the part that matters most," Marco said. "One of the guards remembers Samantha arguing with Jeremiah, telling him to back off. He thinks Jeremiah tried to hit on her, and she shot him down."

"And he couldn't take it," Maya said, excitement building in her at the news. Suddenly, it seemed that she might have found a clear motive for the guard, to go with his lack of an alibi, his propensity for violence, and his presence at all four prisons.

"Maybe that's how it happened with all the others," Marco suggested. "He started by harassing them, and then it escalated."

It sounded plausible. More than plausible. It was definitely enough to hold Jeremiah while they looked for more.

"Thank you, Marco, you've done a great job," Maya said.

He'd found enough evidence to corroborate the kind of man Jeremiah was. It was enough to convince Maya about him. She walked back inside, and found Sheriff Recks waiting with Jeremiah by his side, still cuffed.

"That call just confirmed plenty of what I've already heard," Maya said. "Jeremiah Wood, we'll be holding you for the murders, along with everything else that comes up once we get your colleagues' testimony down on paper."

"Not here, you won't," Sheriff Recks said.

Maya couldn't keep her dislike off her face. "Then I'll drive him back to the prison and see if they have a cell to put him in. If that doesn't work, I'll take him to Alexandria. This is happening, Sheriff."

She grabbed Jeremiah, pulling him away from his buddy.

"What are you waiting for, Sheriff?" Jeremiah said. "Arrest her!"

Maya ignored him, dragging him to the car. However much the sheriff might dislike it, she'd done it. She'd found the man who had killed Samantha Neele.

132

CHAPTER TWENTY FOUR

Frank sat in the control room of his bunker, watching, listening, waiting. He pieced together the world from different sources, feeds telling him what was happening, suggesting what *might* happen.

Currently, they were telling him that Agent Grey had brought in a man for the murder of Samantha Neele.

He'd looked at her face, heard the confidence in her voice. She believed it. She was sure that she'd found the right person. And, looking at it, Frank had to admit that her belief made a lot of sense. By any objective standard, Jeremiah Wood was an awful man, a danger to women. He certainly did not treat them with the care and love that Frank showed to his bunnies.

Frank could see the way the evidence fit together. He could see the pieces of the jigsaw slotting into place in his head. That had always been one of his gifts. He'd known from a young age that he was more intelligent than the ordinary people around him. He'd always known that he didn't see the world in the limited ways they did. That he was special.

Now, he could see the lines that led Agent Grey through to the arrest she'd just made. Making the connection between the four guards was a nice leap, one that many people wouldn't have thought to look for. Realizing that this couldn't be someone's first kill showed a knowledge of her craft. Even when she'd been proven wrong that first time, dear Maya hadn't given up. She'd gone back and thought things through to find a new angle. She'd found a guard who fit every piece of evidence that she had so far.

It was just a pity, really, that she was wrong.

Frank sat there in front of his screens, considering what to do about that fact. And it *was* a fact. Frank had deduced it himself, and he didn't have the constraints of the law when it came to gaining his information. That was one tie that would always hold dear Maya back, until she learned better.

Perhaps he should teach her that lesson now. He looked over to where the large timer was ticking down, still with plenty of time left on it. Perhaps he shouldn't say anything until the deadline, then leave a postcard carefully explaining the dangers of jumping to conclusions, clutched in the dead hands of the bunny who died for Agent Grey's mistake.

That was tempting, but there were other options.

As he considered them, Frank put on his mask and strolled through to the main part of his underground complex. The bunnies were mostly scattered and out of sight, but he caught a glimpse of one, just flitting around a corner.

"Stay!" he commanded.

Sure enough, when he went around the corner, the bunny was there, a pretty little red haired thing, looking at him with big round eyes, tears already falling down her cheeks in her terror. Amusing that in spite of that terror, she should stand so still. Did she fear the consequences of disobedience so much?

Good.

"I have a question to ask you," Frank said. "A... moral quandary, if you will."

Frank normally didn't have problems with such things. He acted in the way that was most advantageous. Anything else was weakness. Now, though, there was a degree of amusement to be had in watching this young woman squirm. It reminded him of the joy that came from watching Maya run like a rat in a maze, although less pronounced.

"My quandary is very simple: should I give dear Maya a clue to help her in her endeavors?"

"A clue?" the bunny echoed.

"A lifeline, if you will. You see, she believes that she has succeeded in the task that I have set for her, yet she is sorely mistaken."

"How... how do you know that?" the bunny managed.

"Isn't it obvious?" Frank asked, and then realized that no, it probably wasn't to her. People were so foolish, sometimes. Oh, and she didn't have half the information that he did, of course.

"I know because I have worked out for myself exactly who has done this. The answer is quite obvious, if you know where to look and have the resources."

"So this is all just a *game* to you?" the bunny demanded.

The mask didn't show Frank's face, but just the intensity of his eyes through it was enough to stop her short. He would not have his pets speak to him in that tone.

134

"You're starting to see the problem," he said. "On the one hand, I would dearly like the truth to come out. I would like Agent Grey to solve the case, and find the truth. Oh, and there is the matter of one of you dying if she does not."

He saw the fear on the young woman's face increase a little. That was better.

"On the other hand, it *is* a game, and games have rules. If I cheat like this… well, I might as well just send her the answer. It makes the whole thing pointless. I might as well just send her the totality of what I know, kill all of you, and let it run from there."

"Why *don't* you do that?" the bunny asked him.

"Where would be the fun in that?" Frank asked. "Besides, as annoying as it is, there are some things even I know only part of. My hope is that an FBI agent on the ground may find out more."

He paused considering the young woman. It would be so easy to reach out and hurt her. Yet that wasn't the way they were playing this. That wasn't the point of any of this.

"Well?" he said. "I'm waiting. Should I give dear Maya her clue?"

"Yes," the bunny managed. "Yes, you should help her."

"Really?" Frank said. "Why?"

He saw her squirming, caught out by that challenge.

"Because it will help to keep your game going," she replied. "It's no fun for you if she just loses."

"Oh, it could be quite enjoyable," Frank said. "For one thing, I would get to kill one of you, watch the light fade from your eyes, listen to the rattle of that last breath."

She took a step back, the terror in her expression obvious.

"Still, you have a point. Very well, I will give her a clue. But if she fails… it will be *you* who pays the price."

CHAPTER TWENTY FIVE

Maya dared to breathe a sigh of relief as she and Marco drove back to Alexandria and their hotel. She'd found a good suspect in Samantha Neele's murder, and with time to spare. She would check the other prisons, and she had no doubt at all that the other dead women would be on the list of those Jeremiah had harassed. She would find a way to get a confession from him, or find physical evidence.

Once she did, she would get a postcard with a location for the woman the kidnapper intended to release, and this time, Maya would ensure that *nothing* happened to her.

She felt triumphant in that moment, like she could do just about anything. Last time, it had felt to Maya as if she'd been scrabbling around in the dark, trying to find answers that weren't there. This time, the answer had been sitting there in front of her all along. All she needed now was a little more proof.

"When we get back to the hotel, I want to put together the papers on the case," Maya said. "I want to call the other prisons, find out about him there, make sure that we have everything in order before I hand it off, so that there's no way of Jeremiah wriggling off the hook."

Maya wanted to make sure that this was solid, and not just because the kidnapper probably wouldn't be happy if Samantha's killer immediately got released. Maya didn't *like* Jeremiah. He was a bully and probably worse, as well as being a killer. She wanted to make sure that anything that could be made to stick to him did so.

"It will be fine," Marco assured her. "Even without the murder charge, some of the stuff his colleagues have started to say might be enough to put him away. Abusing prisoners just because he can? Some of the things he's done to female guards? Once a jury hears all of it, there's no way that they won't convict."

Maya hoped so, but she wanted to make certain. That was why, as soon as they got back to the hotel, she got her laptop out and started to work through it all again. The first thing she did was send what she had so far through to Harris and the others at the FBI. She didn't want the first he heard about all this to be on the news.

After that, Maya started to piece together Jeremiah Wood's career, starting with the moment he signed up to be a prison guard at age eighteen. A note on his file referred to the army, and Maya did her best to trace those records. It helped that she still had some of her contacts from her time in the army, and Maya put a message through to one of them, explaining the situation.

A few minutes later, a file pinged back to her. It was brief, because Jeremiah hadn't served for very long. In fact, it looked as though he'd been kicked out of basic training on psychological grounds. Apparently, his bullying and his attitude had been too much even for the army, or maybe they just had enough drill sergeants already.

From there, it seemed that he'd gone into his first prison, and even though it was years ago now, Maya put in a call.

"Hello, is this the East Valley correctional facility? My name is Agent Maya Grey, with the FBI. I'm hoping to speak to someone about one of your former employees, Jeremiah Wood. He would have worked there perhaps six years ago? Around the time of the murder of one of your guards. Yes, I'll hold."

Maya waited.

"Hello?" a voice on the other end of the line said. "This is Warden Smithers. I understand that you want to talk about one of our former guards."

"Jeremiah Wood," Maya said. "I want to know what sort of man he was, and anything you remember about him from around the time of the murder of Justine Kells. Do you remember him?"

"I do," the warden said. "But I don't like speaking ill of my former employees, even if…"

"Even if what?" Maya asked. "I should tell you that Jeremiah has just been arrested on suspicion of the murder of four guards, including Justine Kells."

"Really?" That seemed to catch the warden by surprise. "Well, in that case, I suppose I should tell you. He left under something of a cloud. There were accusations about the way he treated prisoners, especially female prisoners. There was never quite enough proof to do anything, but eventually, we had to ask him to leave."

"And there was no mention of it on his record," Maya said.

"Well, without proof…"

Without proof, they just sent him onto the next place, to become someone else's problem.

137

"Do you remember him around the time of the murder?" Maya asked. "Did he argue with Justine Kells?"

"I... there were some suggestions that they had argued." the warden said. "I believe she had told him to back off with the prisoners. I don't really know the details. After so long, I only have a general impression of the man."

"Did his behavior seem different after her death? Did he do anything or make any comments that seem more important now that he's been arrested?"

"Not that I remember," the warden said.

"I understand," Maya said. "Thank you for your time. If you think of anything, please call me back, and we may need to interview anyone who worked with him at a later point."

She sat there and tapped her fingers together for a few seconds.

"Something wrong?" Marco asked. He seemed to be wading through Jeremiah's personnel files, circling anything that might be of interest.

"I'm not sure," Maya said. "It's just... Jeremiah isn't very good at hiding his emotions. He's not the kind of guy who could smile to your face and plot something. Yet his former boss didn't notice any change in him after the murder of Justine Kells."

"Maybe he just didn't see him day to day?" Marco suggested, which was almost exactly what the prison warden had said.

"Maybe," Maya said, but she still didn't feel entirely happy.

It was a surprising feeling. An hour ago, and she would have said that nothing could dent her certainty that Jeremiah was the killer. Everything about him screamed that he had to be. Maya had found the link between him and the prisons, after all.

Yet even that seemed a little too easy. Surely he would have realized that someone would find the connection between the dead prison guards sooner or later. Was he that arrogant that he thought no one would realize that he had been at the same prisons as all four?

Maybe he was. Jeremiah was definitely arrogant, definitely violent, definitely had the kind of hatred for female authority figures that might propel him to do something like this.

"You don't sound too certain," Marco said.

"I'll just feel happier when we find one piece of concrete evidence to back up the rest of this," Maya said. "I want the knife that he used. The wounds on all four victims were the same, and there was no

138

weapon at the scene, so that says to me that the killer kept the knife around. If we find that, then the case is airtight."

"It's pretty strong, anyway," Marco said. "We'll get a conviction. You don't need to worry, Maya."

And yet, Maya *was* worrying. Before, everything had felt fine, but now... now there was a nagging doubt at the back of her mind.

It was still there when Harris called her.

"Sir?" she said, picking up.

"You made an arrest in the case?"

"Yes sir," Maya began. "Although-"

"Well done, Grey. And well inside the kidnapper's deadline this time, too. Have you heard any news from him?"

"Not yet, sir," Maya said. "It's just-"

"I should notify you that I've just had calls through from the Pollock Sheriff's Department, making a formal complaint about you, Grey."

The switch of topic caught Maya a little off guard, but honestly, the complaint was nothing Maya hadn't expected.

"The sheriff objects to me making him look bad ahead of his re-election," Maya said. "Apparently, I should have left Johnathan Dennis in prison."

"The complaint says that you have been consistently confrontational, have sought out conflict with his department, have involved a police officer without jurisdiction in your investigation, and have held an innocent man even though the sheriff *ordered* you not to. Is that correct, Agent Grey?"

It wasn't Harris' sternest tone. Instead, there was a weariness to it, obviously wondering why he had to deal with all this from some local sheriff. Maya knew the feeling.

"Pretty much," Maya said. "Although it does miss out the part where he tried to obstruct my investigation at every turn, falsified a complaint about a stolen vehicle to try to get me arrested, and is drinking buddies with the man in question. Oh, and Marco is here to back me up. It's still my investigation."

"In which case, I don't think there's too much to worry about," Harris said. "We'll have to look into it once you get back here, but for now, keep doing what you're doing. Detective Spinelli is proving helpful?"

Maya was surprised he wasn't objecting more strongly to Marco's presence.

"I couldn't have done any of this without him," she said.

"Good. I'm glad I suggested to his superiors that he take a little time off. And suggested to him that it might be good to see this through."

Maya froze. "You did *what*?"

"Did you think the Cleveland PD did it out of the goodness of their hearts?" Harris asked. "You need a partner, Grey, and Detective Spinelli is the only person I've seen you work alongside willingly. If this goes well, maybe we'll have to see about getting him a transfer."

"Harris, that is…" Maya wasn't even sure that she had the words for just how manipulative her boss could be.

"Exactly what I needed to do?" Harris suggested. "In the meantime, I think we counter these complaints with a few of our own. I don't care if I can't actually have the sheriff's badge for everything he's done, I'm not letting anyone just get away with making life that difficult for one of my agents. It sets a bad precedent for whoever you work with next. How soon are you going to wrap things up there?"

"I still have more evidence to collect on Jeremiah Wood," Maya said.

"You can do that from here. Come back to DC. We'll deal with everything once you're back at the office. In the meantime, keep me posted."

Harris hung up, leaving Maya without a chance to express any of her doubts. She found herself looking over at Marco, feeling strange now that she knew that he was basically only able to be there because Harris was playing professional matchmaker. That made Maya feel a little uncomfortable, when things had never felt uncomfortable with Marco before.

"What is it?" Marco asked.

"Harris wants me back at the office," Maya said. "As far as he's concerned, all of this is wrapped up, bar the lawyers."

"He has a point," Marco said. "I know it would be nice to have some more direct evidence, but with Jeremiah, you've got motive, means, and opportunity. Add in all the stuff that's starting to come out about him, and there's no way a jury will be able to keep from convicting."

Maya hoped that it would be that simple. She wanted this to be an open and shut case. It was just-

"Excuse me, Agent?" one of the hotel staff came forward, holding a by now familiar bunny patterned rectangle in her hand. "This postcard just arrived, addressed to you."

Relief flooded through Maya at the sight of it. It meant that they'd finished this. It meant that another woman would be safe. She took it gratefully, daring to relax for the first time in days.

At the same time, the arrival brought up all the worries she had about the kidnapper being able to monitor her. Somehow, he was completely up to the minute on her investigation. He knew exactly where to find her, and what she was doing. That was a terrifying thought in itself.

"Did you see who brought it?" Maya asked.

"Just a courier. He was wearing a motorcycle helmet, so I didn't see much else."

Meaning it could have been anyone. Certainly, it wouldn't be easy to track them down now. Even so, Maya ran out, trying to catch a glimpse of them, but by the time she got outside, there was no sign of any courier.

Marco caught up to her.

"What does it say?" he asked. "Is it a location for the pickup of the woman?"

Maya had yet to read the postcard, so she held it up to the light to look at it. The words there made her blood run cold.

Try again, dear Maya. The clock is still ticking, and a life depends on it. Look inside for answers.

The kidnapper didn't think she'd arrested the right person. Which meant... either he was wrong about this, or *Maya* had gone wrong somewhere.

Now, she needed to work out the truth of it, and fast, because the countdown to the deadline was still running.

CHAPTER TWENTY SIX

Maya paced the hotel room, trying to make sense of the postcard that the kidnapper had sent. The message was clear, but it still took a little effort to believe it.

"What does it say?" Marco asked.

"It says that we got it wrong. That Jeremiah isn't the killer."

Marco looked puzzled by that. "But he *fits*. Everything about him fits. He was at all four prisons at the same time. He obviously has problems with women, and-"

"And it isn't him," Maya said. "The kidnapper seems certain of it."

"And how does *he* know?" Marco asked.

That was a good question. How did the kidnapper know better than Maya who the killer was? Was he really able to work out something that Maya couldn't? What extra information did he have?

"It's possible that he has criminal connections we don't," Maya suggested. "And if he's willing to monitor the police, maybe he has other electronic resources. Ones that aren't legal. We already know that he's intelligent."

That made Marco look even less happy about the situation. "So he's… what? Some combination of Sherlock Holmes and the NSA?"

That was a terrifying thought, and it made Maya wonder just who they were dealing with. This was a man who could predict the moves of the FBI perfectly, who seemed to be able to get information on the cases almost instantly, who could point Maya at cases that seemed either settled or just dead, in the knowledge that there was an answer waiting for her.

It pointed to a very frightening kind of individual, one Maya definitely didn't want her sister to be in the hands of. The thought of her there made Maya feel sick.

"Could he be wrong?" Marco asked.

"I…" Maya considered that possibility. She thought about the lack of physical evidence. "I'm not sure he is. Look at the case against Jeremiah. It's persuasive, but everything is circumstantial. As much as I might want it to be him, I'm not Sheriff Recks. If the evidence points another way, we have to go with it."

"What evidence, though?" Marco took a seat. "All we have is the word of a criminal."

"In a way, it's the only thing that matters." That was the worst part of it. "We're doing this to try to satisfy the kidnapper. If he doesn't believe the results, then a woman's life is still in danger, regardless of what we think."

Marco looked about as frustrated as Maya felt. His hands closed into fists on the table, and Maya could pick out the tension around his eyes.

"Does this mean that all of this is just a game? That he has all of the answers waiting, and we just try to keep up? Is this all just about him showing how much cleverer than us he is?"

That was one possibility. That she and Marco were rats running in a maze for the kidnapper's amusement.

"I don't think it's that," Maya said. "I think maybe that's a part of it, and he obviously knows more than we do, but I think maybe more of it is that he wants the truth to come out. He wants us to find evidence, to prove what happened. And obviously, he can't arrest anyone."

"So we're the hands and he's the brains?" Marco said. "Why not just *give* us the answer?"

They both knew the answer to that: because there *was* an element of making them perform for the kidnapper's amusement. Because he was back there somewhere watching, playing a game with them.

It was just that it was a game that would save lives, and see killers brought to justice.

"We need to go back through the evidence," Maya said. "We need to look through it all again."

"What do you expect to find?" Marco asked.

"Something that we missed. Something that we didn't see when we looked before. There has to be something, or why would the kidnapper point us back at this again?"

Maya went to her computer, pulling up the files. She was still convinced that the links between the four dead women were the way to get to the heart of this. It didn't seem in doubt that Samantha Neele had been only the most recent victim of a serial killer.

The question now was who else that could have been, besides Jeremiah.

143

"So, we know that there are no prisoners on the parole lists who could have done it," Maya said. "And we know that there are no guards besides Jeremiah who were at all four prisons. That's right, isn't it?"

"According to the files. We can check them again."

They did, because Maya didn't want to put a woman's life in danger just because she hadn't read through the personnel files properly. As well as running searches on them, this time, she read through every name, making sure that there wasn't someone left off because of some small difference in spelling, or some quirk of the search program. A computer might assume that there were two different people when in fact there was only a small difference between their names.

There was nothing like that, though, and Maya could feel her frustration starting to build. If it weren't for the kidnapper's postcard, she would have assumed that she'd gotten everything right. It was frustrating to know that somewhere in all this, she'd gone wrong, but not to be able to see where.

"Is it possible that there were guards who worked at one or more of the prisons but weren't on the list?" Maya asked Marco. "Is it possible that they took some on as contract workers, that someone could have worked there temporarily and not make it onto the main staff lists?"

"There are already some temporary workers on there," Marco pointed out. "But I can check with the prisons if you like, make a couple of calls and see if it's possible."

Maya nodded. "Please."

Marco went over to the other side of the room, starting to make the calls. For her part, Maya tried to think of other ways that someone might have met all four women. Did prison guards train in the same places? Did they go to industry conferences? Was there a support group somewhere for female prison guards where they could all talk about their experiences, and someone was targeting the members of that?

Maya started to look into each of those possibilities. The notion that the four women had trained together was a non-starter. Corrections officers seemed to get their training through the facilities that they worked in, working to whatever standard the facility required. In any case, Samantha and the others had all been different ages, and had all started their careers at different times.

Was it possible that they'd been on a training course somewhere together? The simple answer was no, because the earliest victim died

144

before Samantha Neele even went into corrections as a career. Was it possible that they'd gone on a course with the same instructor at different times?

That was more plausible, but it was relatively straightforward to check, because the women's files held details of their resumes and work. Maya started to wade through them, and couldn't find a single point of connection.

"How are things going over there?" she asked Marco. If he came back and said that yes, the prisons used temporary workers, she could start to track down the agencies they used and ask who their staff had been. It would take time, but that kind of work was what found answers.

"The first two prisons have both said that any staff have to go on their official staff records, even if they're only there temporarily," Marco said, sounding as tired as Maya felt. He'd been through the same rollercoaster of emotions that she had, thinking that they'd found an answer, only to have it snatched away.

"Which means it can't be that." Maya was starting to run out of ideas. This kind of wading through possibilities was normal for cold case work, but she had the feeling that none of these options were what the kidnapper had in mind when he told her that she was on the wrong track.

What *did* he have in mind? Maya picked up the postcard, turning it over and over in her hands. Previously, the kidnapper had hidden his hints and traps in the message. He'd included the first case only as the return address on the postcard, and had been able to set up an attempt to trace it in such a way that it led straight into a trap. Could there be something on here that Maya wasn't seeing?

The picture on the front was one of eleven hopping bunnies, with no obvious differences from the previous postcards beyond the number. Even that was presumably a reference to the number of remaining captives rather than anything to do with this case.

The message on the back was opaque, almost meaningless. Maya should look inside? Was the kidnapper telling her that she should look at her own feelings on this for an answer? If so, it was the kind of help that just *wasn't* helpful. Telling her to look inwards and trust her feelings achieved nothing.

A second idea came to Maya even as she thought that.

"Marco, do you have a knife? Pocket knife, anything?"

Marco reached into his belt and pulled out a Swiss Army knife, handing it over. Using it, Maya carefully pried apart the layers of the postcard, trying to see if there was anything hidden within. It would be exactly the kidnapper's style to leave a clue set out neatly in between two layers laminated together. The only result of her efforts, though, was a mess of torn paper left on the table she was using for her laptop and a slightly disapproving look from one of the hotel's staff.

What else, what else? What did the kidnapper mean? He had to think that it was sufficient extra information to solve this. So what did "Look inside" mean? Inside… inside…

Maya froze as the answer hit her. She'd been looking at prisons for days now. In that context, inside meant only one thing.

"Damn it, I've made a mistake," Maya said, hurrying to her laptop.

"What mistake?" Marco asked.

"It's a prisoner."

Marco looked very doubtful. "We *looked* at prisoners."

Maya shook her head. "We looked at the parole files. That means prisoners who are *out* of prison. What if our killer is still in prison somewhere?"

She saw the realization of the truth dawn on Marco's face.

"I'm still thinking like a homicide detective, like the murder is going to be out there making a run for it," Marco said. "You're right. This happened long enough ago that the killer could be in prison for something else by now."

Maya was already searching through prison records, switching away from the parole files, looking at current inmates. Had anyone been in all four of the prisons? A name stood out: Ade Matheson. Maya didn't rush into anything this time. Instead, she took her time, reading his file carefully.

There were a lot of similarities to Augustine Harmer. He'd been in the same prisons, at more or less the same time. Only *his* convictions all seemed to be for violence against women, when he'd raised his hand to girlfriends and partners, attacked them at home, battered them simply because he could. He was a man who clearly had no problem using violence to get what he wanted.

His current conviction was the one that sealed it for Maya. Six months ago, down in Alexandria, he'd murdered his neighbor, a young woman. He'd been found by the victim's boyfriend, standing over her corpse more or less as J.D. had been, with blood on his hands.

146

Only in his case, there was no doubt that he'd done it.

He was currently serving life without parole for that killing, and serving it in the Pollock Correctional Facility.

"We've found him," Maya said, but stopped herself before she got too excited this time.

She wanted proof. She wanted to be certain that she'd gotten the right man. That meant exactly one thing.

"We need to set up a meeting with Ade Matheson. I want to look him in the eyes and hear it for myself. I want a confession."

CHAPTER TWENTY SEVEN

The last time Maya had been in the prison's interview room, with its bolted down furniture and its metal table, she had been there to meet J.D. She'd been unconvinced about his guilt and he'd shuffled in a broken man.

None of that was true with the man she'd come to meet today. From the moment Maya saw Ade Matheson, she was sure that she'd gotten it right this time. Ade Matheson strode in spite of the shackles that confined him, wearing the orange of his jumpsuit as proudly as if it were the finest tailoring. The guards beside him seemed almost to keep their distance from him, as if afraid that he might lash out at them.

He was a tall man, muscled in the way that came from too much time in prison: all upper body, everything proclaiming his ability to hit hard if anyone got into his space. His head was shaven, but he had a short, dark beard, while his features had a puffiness to them that came from too many drugs, too much fighting, or both. He stood in front of the table, not sitting down.

"A woman? The FBI sent a *woman*?" He made it sound like some kind of terrible insult.

"A woman who has worked out what you've done, Mr. Matheson," Maya said. "I'm Agent Grey, with the FBI cold cases unit. Why don't you sit down and we'll talk about the crimes you *haven't* been convicted of yet?"

Marco was more direct. "Sit down. Now."

The look Matheson shot their way was cold, devoid of anything approaching empathy or kindness. Maya had seen looks like that before, in pictures and videos from her training, when they'd been talking to the worst kind of killers, trying to understand them and their patterns.

"You said that you wanted to talk," Matheson said. "Well, I'm not saying anything with him here. Or the guards. You want answers, you only get them if it's just you and me."

"We can't allow that, ma'am," one of the guards said. "Matheson is dangerous."

148

Maya probably knew exactly how dangerous better than they did.

"I know," she said. "But I still need the room. I assume the recorder can stay on, Mr. Matheson?"

He shrugged. "I don't care about that."

He just wanted her alone in there with him. Maya nodded.

"All right, everyone else wait outside."

Marco didn't look happy. "You're sure?"

"I am," Maya said.

"Ok, but if I hear *anything* going wrong, I'm coming in."

The guards nodded and took Matheson to the table before they left. Marco was the last one out, giving the prisoner what Maya assumed was a warning look.

"He wants to protect you," Matheson said. "I assume you're sleeping with him?"

"What? No," Maya retorted.

"Nonsense. That's how bitches like you get what you want. You sleep with men; you wrap them around your fingers. You slide up into positions of authority without ever *earning* them. You act as if you're in charge of the world."

"Is that why you feel the need to be violent towards women, Ade?" Maya asked. "To show us our place?"

"So confident," Matheson said. "So secure because you have me on the wrong side of some restraints. You think I couldn't get across that table and hurt you, little agent?"

Maya forced down the fear she felt in the face of Matheson's hostility. That was what he wanted from her.

"I think if you could do it, you would have, by now. I think you like hurting women in positions of authority too much."

"There is no evidence of that, Agent," Matheson said.

"No evidence that you're a killer?" Maya said. She gave the room around them a pointed look.

"My whore of a neighbor was like you, always running her mouth, trying to be clever," Matheson said.

"Is that why you stabbed her?" Maya asked. It wasn't the thing she'd come here to talk about, but she wanted to gauge how Matheson reacted when he talked about his crimes.

"She made me angry."

"Angry enough that they found you standing over her corpse with a knife in your hands and blood all over you," Maya observed.

149

She watched the lack of expression in response to that from the prisoner opposite her. What he'd done didn't touch him. He was obviously capable of anger and possibly of other emotional responses, but he didn't show the slightest trace of guilt or understanding when it came to his crime.

She was dealing with a psychopath.

"*You're* starting to make me angry, Agent Grey," Matheson said.

"Angry enough that you'll sneak into my house at night, stab me in my kitchen, then leave, taking the knife with you?"

Maya set those words down carefully, wanting to see Matheson's reaction. Again, there was no guilt, no remorse. His face was blank, but the kind of blank that seemed more of a defensive wall to Maya.

"I don't know what you're talking about," Matheson said, but there was no outrage there, no surprise.

Maya was sure in that moment that he was lying, but now she had to break that lie down. Because after the way she'd failed with the prison guard, no one was going to convict him of the murder on just her word.

"Samantha Neele. Before that, Kelly Brooker, Adawe Ali, and Justine Kells," Maya said.

"I don't know those names," Matheson said.

"Of course you do," Maya replied. "You were in prisons where all of them were guards."

"I should know the guards' names?" Matheson demanded, but now Maya could see a flicker of worry there. Or was it anger?

"I think you knew their names," Maya said. "I think you hated having women as guards there, with power over you. Isn't that right, Ade?"

"You don't know *anything*," he said.

"I know that you were out of prison at the time of each of the killings. I know that you're the only one *left* who has a connection to all four women."

"Why would I do something like that?" Matheson asked.

Maya stared at him, trying to find a way in below that exterior, that smug confidence, backed up by a total disdain for her and any other woman he met. Maya saw that, and she knew what she had to do. There was only one way that she was going to get the truth out of Matheson, but it was dangerous, very dangerous.

"How does it feel to know that a woman beat you?" she asked.

150

"You haven't done-"

She cut him off, because she knew that would only rile him more. "I have, and frankly, it wasn't that hard. You think you're some kind of ghost, who's never left a trace, but you were found standing over a body by accident, because you couldn't do basic surveillance properly. Now, I've found *this* connection, and it took me what? A few days? You're not very good at this, are you, Ade?"

"Shut up, bitch."

"Why? Are you going to do to me what you did to the guards? Are you going to kill me in my own home? Did they laugh at you, Matheson, trapped there behind bars? Trapped like you're trapped now? Did you feel so powerless that you had to do something?"

"Shut *up*!"

"I'm going to prove that it was you, Ade. I'm going to drag you in front of a court, prove this, and there's *nothing* you can do to stop it."

"I said shut up!" Matheson roared, and lunged at her.

The speed of it was impressive. In spite of his shackles, Matheson moved forward fast enough that Maya had no time to dodge as he dove at her over the table. He slammed into her and they both went tumbling to the ground.

Matheson came up on top, his weight bearing down on her. Maya fought back, but he was stronger, and now his shackles were a weapon, pressing against Maya's throat, cutting off her air.

"You think you're clever? You're nothing!" he snarled. "Just like *they* were nothing. Standing the other side of the bars, sneering at me."

Maya clawed at his hands, but it wasn't the hands that were the problem.

"I watched them. I went to their houses. I made them see how weak they were when I killed them. And now you want to talk about me getting things wrong? I disappeared. I did it *perfectly*!"

His weight bore down on Maya, making her vision go dark at the edges as the lack of oxygen cut into her brain. She had the admission that she wanted, but was it going to cost her life?

No, she couldn't let that happen. She wouldn't. Not when her sister was still in danger.

Summoning the last strength she had, Maya trapped one of Matheson's arms, then bucked and rolled coming up on top of him. Without his weight pressing down into her throat, she could breathe again, but he was still fighting, still lashing out at her. Maya reared up and threw a punch, catching him badly, but still managing to make some room. Matheson tried to drag Maya back down, but she went with the movement instead of fighting it, slipping past his legs, driving her knee into his sternum to hold him down. She threw another couple of punches as he struggled, and *that* bought her the room she needed to back away.

Even as she did it, Marco and the guards came piling into the room, grabbing Matheson and hauling him to his feet.

"Please tell me that the recorder got all that," Maya said, rubbing her throat as Matheson struggled to get free.

"We heard it all," Marco said. "Grey, that was-"

"What I needed to do to get a confession." She smiled over at Matheson. "I knew Ade here wouldn't be able to stand the thought of a woman getting the better of him."

"Bitch! I'll kill you! I'll cut you to pieces. You'll never be safe."

"I'm perfectly safe," Maya said. "Because you're never getting out of here."

Matheson glowered at Maya as she dusted herself off. Then she heard him laugh, his whole expression changing.

"Agent Grey, you're forgetting one thing."

"What's that?" Maya asked, turning back to him anyway.

"I was never getting out of here *anyway*. You think you've put a dangerous killer away? You haven't. You haven't *caught* me. That happened by accident, and it was a man who did it. Tell me, how does it feel to know that everything you've done here is for nothing? How does it feel to just be *less*?"

Those words caught Maya by surprise. She hadn't thought of that side of things.

"I knew before I walked into this room that I would be spending the rest of my life in this prison," Matheson said. "That hasn't changed. Will there even be a trial for all of this? If there is, it's a nice day out for me, getting to go to the courtroom, getting to wear something other than prison orange. Maybe I'll even plead innocent, just so that you have to come down and testify. Maybe I'll represent myself, and I'll get to ask you all *kinds* of questions on the stand. Even if they shut me up, it will still waste your time, and taxpayer money."

He sounded as though he was enjoying his petty idea of revenge.

"And for what?" he asked. "So they add another four life sentences. So what? I only live and die once. In here, making the jump from killer to mass murderer? That's an *increase* in status. People will be even more scared of me. You've done me a favor, Agent Grey."

A favor? Maya couldn't imagine someone who thought of it like that, yet, maybe, here in prison, it was exactly that. It paid to be the biggest, scariest guy out there, and nothing said "scary" like being a serial killer. One who killed guards, especially.

Which made Maya wonder what the point of all this was. She'd been so determined through this, and had felt so excited in the moment when she'd worked out the truth, yet Maya could feel that excitement ebbing away now. She'd put so much work into this, put up with so much from the local sheriff and his cronies, all to get to this point.

What was going to change, though? She'd caught a man who was already in prison, a man who didn't even seem to care that Maya had found out the truth. All that effort, and what did it count for?

Maya walked out of the room with Marco in her wake, feeling dejected. She could hear Matheson laughing behind her in triumph. She shook her head.

"Let's get out of here. I'm done with this town."

CHAPTER TWENTY EIGHT

Maya drove back to Pollock, and while she did it, she and Marco had to give a ride to the one person she really didn't want to.

"I'm going to have your job for wrongly arresting me, Agent," Jeremiah Wood said.

They'd had to release him now that they knew who the real killer was. Maya disliked that almost as much as the other outcomes of this case.

"No, you won't," Marco snapped at him from the passenger seat. "You want to know why? Because you're going to be too busy finding a new job. Not to mention defending the charges that will probably be brought against you."

"You've got nothing," Jeremiah replied.

"On the murders, maybe, but the moment you were out of the picture, people started to open up about everything *else* you've been doing. Last I heard, abusing inmates and harassing staff was a crime."

Maya glanced in the rearview mirror and caught the worry on Jeremiah's face. She was glad of that. It meant that they'd done *some* small good here. They'd definitely achieved more than they had by finding Ade Matheson.

"Drop me off at the sheriff's station," Jeremiah said, which instantly tempted Maya to simply stop the car and make him walk the rest of the way.

She didn't, though, because she had a couple of things to say to the sheriff when she saw him, too. She also had something very specific that she wanted to do when she met him. When she got closer, she sent a message through to Harris, and then made a call.

They pulled up outside the sheriff's station in Pollock, and the sheriff came out to meet them, accompanied by several of his men.

"What are you doing back here?" he demanded.

"Returning your drinking buddy," Maya said. "Turns out he wasn't a killer, just an A-grade asshole who's going to face charges for the way he treated prisoners."

"So you were wrong!" Sheriff Recks said, looking triumphant.

"I was," Maya said. "And unlike you, I can admit that. But it took *evidence* to show it, not just the word of some good old boy sheriff."

"At least *I* managed to get a suspect convicted for the killings," Sheriff Recks shot back.

"You're proud of getting the wrong man convicted?" Maya said. She looked over to Jeremiah. "You two deserve one another. Oh, and I should probably say that I have a full confession from the real killer. A man who went on to kill again because *you* didn't catch him at the time."

This was petty, but it was making Maya feel better, not least because it reminded her that she'd done some good on this case. The real killer might already be in prison, but at least an innocent man had walked free.

She could see the anger starting to build on Sheriff Recks's face. "If you're done here, I want you out of my town. If you're still here in another hour, FBI or not, I'll find something to arrest you on."

"On what evidence?" Maya asked.

"I'll *find* evidence. Even if I have to plant it myself."

"Thank you," Maya said. She took out her phone, where the line had been open all this time, and put it on speaker. "Sir, is that enough?"

"It's enough to get things rolling," Harris said. "I'm sure we'll find far more once an investigative team gets down there."

Maya could see the shock and surprise on Sheriff Recks's face.

"That... that's entrapment. Illegal recording. None of that will stand up in court!"

Maya smiled back at him. "You're missing the point, Sheriff. It doesn't *have* to stand up in court. It just has to make enough noise to lose you your precious re-election campaign."

"You-"

"I'd consider what you say and do next very carefully, Sheriff," Maya said, as she went back to the car. "The line is still open."

She got in. Sure, she and Marco would have to leave in a hurry now, but Maya hadn't been planning on hanging around in any case. She'd done everything she'd come here to do. Now, she needed to get back to DC.

"Why are you looking so down about all this?" Marco asked.

"It's just the pointlessness of it," Maya said. "The kidnapper has sent us on this grand chase after a killer, and it turns out to be a guy who is already in prison. A guy who the kidnapper clearly *knew* was the killer, or else how would he be able to send me the clue that solved all of this?"

Marco shook his head. "You're looking at this the wrong way, Maya."

"What's the right way to look at it?"

"Well, for one thing, you *have* solved the case. That means that a woman somewhere is going to be safe who wouldn't be otherwise. That's a big deal."

It was, of course it was. It was just that it felt that, instead of doing some good while they were solving the case, all they'd accomplished was to jump through the hoops the kidnapper had set out for them.

"Then there's the fact that J.D. gets to walk free," Marco pointed out. "That's a big deal too. An innocent man is out there now who would be rotting in prison otherwise."

"I doubt that's the reason the kidnapper sent us," Maya said, as they made their way towards Alexandria.

"That part doesn't matter. What matters is that you've managed to do something good, something that will make a difference. Then there's all the corruption that you've uncovered. The town might get a sheriff and a head prison guard who deserve the roles."

"Maybe," Maya said, although Marco's positivity was starting to pull her out of the negative spiral that she'd been dipping into.

"And even without all that, you found the truth," Marco said. "Samantha's mother will get to know what really happened to her daughter. This will have an end to it. Isn't that a big part of your job?"

It was probably the biggest part, certainly the reason that Maya did the job. Put like that, it sounded like she'd actually accomplished a lot. Even with the killer sitting in prison already, not caring about what happened next, the rest of it had to count for something.

As they drove, Maya wished that she could say that she would miss Louisiana, but mostly, getting out of there meant that she wouldn't have to spend her time looking over her shoulder for the cops.

"So, I thought maybe we should talk about before, when we nearly... you know," Marco said as they drove towards the airport. He looked slightly apprehensive, like he'd been thinking about this for most of the journey.

"What's there to talk about?" Maya said. "I get it. You want to keep things professional while we're working together."

156

"Yeah, about that. It occurs to me that we've *finished* working together now."

That stopped Maya short. She'd gotten so used to having Marco by her side that it hadn't occurred to her that in just a few minutes, he would be heading back to Cleveland, her to Washington, and then they might not see one another again.

"So I was wondering," Marco said. "Maybe you could come over to Cleveland again sometime, or I could come to DC. You could show me around? Maybe we could get dinner?"

"You're asking me out on a date?" Maya said. After the way Marco had wanted to keep things professional, the whole suggestion caught her a little by surprise.

"Would that be so bad?" Marco asked, looking faintly amused.

"No, that would be... that would be great. I'd like that," Maya said. "I mean, if you're sure that it's going to be ok?"

"My vacation days are going to run out soon," Marco said. "I figure that this is the only way I get to see more of you. Yes, I'm sure."

The idea of actually getting to go out to dinner somewhere with Marco was a pleasant one. The idea of everything that might happen after that was sufficiently distracting such that Maya had to force herself to keep her eyes on the road rather than on him.

They got to the airport, and from there they had to go through all the tedious business of returning Maya's rental car, arranging to have Marco's picked up, then making sure they knew where their flights were. Marco's was in just a few minutes, so Maya went over with him as far as the security of the airport allowed. She stood there outside the departure gate, ready to see him off.

"Don't worry, Grey," he said, as he turned to get on his flight. "This isn't going to be the last you'll see of me."

Maya hoped not. Even so, she felt a little surprised by just how much she was looking forward to the next time she saw him, even as he stepped onto his flight. She'd started all of this determined that she didn't need anyone to help her, and now, she found herself wishing that Marco wasn't going.

Maya had to head over to her own flight then, waiting in the departure lounge with all the families and business people heading back to DC. She amused herself by trying to guess at the jobs of the different people there, working out who obviously worked in politics or for some government agency, who was just going there on vacation. After days

157

of pushing herself to try to think of answers, it was nice to have a moment to relax.

As she did so, though, Maya found another thought intruding on her growing calm. She'd found things to make this case meaningful to her. She'd remembered the importance of what she did to the innocent, to the families of the dead, and even just to herself in terms of knowing the truth. What, though, was the kidnapper's stake in all of this?

Maya doubted that he had much of an interest in justice; and even if he did, he'd *known* that the real killer was sitting behind bars. If all he wanted was to make the world a safer place out of some twisted vigilante instinct, then why pick a case where the culprit was already off the streets?

So, not that. Likewise, Maya couldn't imagine someone who was prepared to kidnap, hurt, and even kill, being in this out of the good of his heart. This wasn't someone trying to bring closure to families, or see to it that justice was done.

Was this about the other things the case had brought about? No, that didn't fit. The last case hadn't seen an innocent man freed, nor had it brought down a corrupt cop. It needed to be something that fit the pattern of both cases, so what had been consistent between them? Both had featured women being killed. Both had been unsolved.

Both had been blamed on the Moonlight Killer.

It had only been briefly in this case, but it had happened. The FBI had considered both this case and the death of Anne Postmartin as possible Moonlight Killer cases, before eventually giving up. If that was the link, if that was the reason that the kidnapper was getting involved, then it couldn't be because they wanted Maya to hunt the Moonlight Killer, because they'd sent her into this knowing exactly who the real culprit was.

That meant... that meant that they wanted her to *exonerate* the Moonlight Killer. They wanted the record set straight about exactly who had committed crimes that had been attributed to the serial killer. Was that about showing that the Moonlight Killer's legend was overrated? Or was it because someone wanted the serial killer's *real* crimes to stand out with all the rumored ones pared away from around them?

Maya could think of only one person who would want that, and the thought of that made her heart pound in her chest, her breath coming

158

short at the thought of exactly who had kidnapped the eleven remaining women.

Her sister was in the hands of the Moonlight Killer.

CHAPTER TWENTY NINE

"Is there a postcard yet?" Harris asked, from across the bullpen of the fourth floor.

Maya flinched at the question he'd asked her half a dozen times today, because she'd seen his frustration rising with each time.

"Not so far, sir."

Maya was as frustrated as he was. It had been a couple of days now, with no news.

Harris's scowl deepened. "Our kidnapper has broken his own rules. We shouldn't have gone along with all of this, Grey. Not if it doesn't even get us back his hostages safely."

Maya hadn't shared her suspicions over exactly who the kidnapper might be. She'd held back partly because she had no way to prove it, but mostly because she was scared of how Harris might react. He'd already put her sister in danger by ordering raids twice. If he learned that it was the Moonlight Killer, then all the resources he had would go into trying to track the postcards' sender down, regardless of the consequences.

Maya wasn't used to not trusting her boss, but here, it didn't feel as though she could.

"We did a lot of good in Pollock," Maya said. "And there's still time for a postcard to show up."

She knew how hard the waiting was, because it wasn't any easier for her. Every moment was torment, the not knowing turning into a slow agony.

"Is there still nothing back on the forensics?" Maya asked.

Harris shook his head. "Not yet. I'm not sure what it would tell us anyway. The identity of a woman we're about to meet? The identity of one who has been attacked by this monster? It's not information that is going to lead us anywhere."

Maya knew he was right, but even so, even a scrap of information was better than nothing. It was definitely better than waiting for something that would only come when the kidnapper, the Moonlight Killer, was ready.

160

The thought of her sister in the hands of a man like that filled every second in between. This was someone who had killed over and over, who clearly had no compunction about doing the vilest things. What had he been doing to Megan wherever he had her? Even if Maya got her back, what kind of scars would an experience like this one leave?

Maya was still worrying about her sister when Reyes ran in, holding a rectangle of card aloft for them to see.

"A postcard came! It has an address!"

Maya looked over to her boss. "No games this time. Please. Not after last time. We don't try to capture him. We just get the woman back safely."

Harris looked as if he might argue with that, but Maya wasn't going to let it go this time. One woman had already died in all this, and several police had been hurt trying to catch the kidnapper. Now that she knew who they were dealing with, it only made Maya more determined not to risk her sister's life.

"All right, we won't lay any kind of trap, we won't go in hot. But we're taking a team. I still think there's a danger that ultimately, all of this is about targeting you."

Now *that* was a frightening thought. That somehow, Maya had caught the Moonlight Killer's attention, and ultimately, it would end with her being his next target.

"For now, the only thing that matters is getting the woman back," Maya said.

*

Harris's idea of not going in hot still involved a full FBI tactical team in a van, an ambulance, and Maya riding along in a car with Harris and Reyes to an address on the outskirts of Washington, where an old house sat, apparently empty. It wasn't as run down as some of the places that the Moonlight Killer had sent them to. To Maya, it looked more like someone had stepped out and left it just a little while ago. It had whitewashed walls and a slate roof, and was set back just far enough from the street that it might have been easy to get someone in there without being seen.

"Remember, this isn't a raid," Maya said as they pulled up. She got out, leading the way, not giving her boss any time to tell her different.

She made it to the door and found it unlocked.

161

"You should let us go first, Agent," one of the tactical team said.

Maya shook her head, though. "He'll be watching, so let's show him that we can stick to his rules for once. All of you, wait out here."

She saw the tactical team leader look over to Harris for confirmation, and the deputy director gave a curt nod.

"Hang back. But I'm coming in with you, Grey. This is still my department, and I'm not letting you go in there alone."

"Sir-"

"No arguments. Everyone else, hang back and watch for movement."

Maya could have stood there arguing with her boss, but there was no time if a woman had been left waiting somewhere in here. If Liza Carty was anything to go by, the woman would have been under considerable physical and mental stress. The sooner Maya got to her, the better.

She took a breath. This was the moment when they would either get a woman back, maybe even her sister back, or be blown to pieces. The hope and the fear fought against one another, and Maya had to push both down, reminding herself that this was her job. This was what she was here to do, whatever the outcome.

She set off into the house with Harris, looking out for the kinds of traps that the Moonlight Killer liked to set for people who blundered in unwarily. There didn't seem to be any tripwires here, though, and there was no sign of the claymore mines he'd used before. Maya couldn't make out any cameras, but she was sure that there would be at least one watching them.

It was obvious that the Moonlight Killer liked to watch her progress.

"Is there anybody here?" Maya called out, because this was a rescue mission, not an attempt to catch the serial killer.

An incoherent moan answered her. Was that a woman's voice, muffled somehow to keep her from calling out?

Maya looked over at Harris, and set off through the house in the direction of the sound.

"Hello?"

Another of those answering sounds, and Maya followed it through the house, into a dining room. Harris took a step forward, and Maya saw the tripwire a fraction too late.

162

"Down!" she yelled in terror, throwing herself to the floor. She heard Harris hit it a moment after she did.

That was the thing, though: she heard it. There was no explosion, no roar of a claymore mine as shrapnel took out the walls around them. Maya lay there, breathing hard for several seconds before she dared to stand up. A handwritten sign seemed to have fallen down because of the tripwire.

Careful, Agent.

"He's playing with us!" Harris snarled, hauling himself to his feet and dusting himself off. "When I get my hands on him…"

Maya understood the feeling. There was almost nothing she wanted more than to get her hands on the Moonlight Killer. Almost. She wanted her sister back more than any of it.

Still, the sound of a woman in obvious discomfort came from the room ahead of her. The dining room was fully furnished, and there were even plates set out on the dining table, as if the owners had walked out while waiting for dinner and not come back.

Or as if someone had set it all up very carefully.

Maya counted eleven place settings.

There, in the middle of the table, was a digital recorder, with the muffled sounds of a woman's voice coming from it. It sat next to an old fashioned toast rack. In it, stuck at a jaunty angle, was a postcard.

Harris obviously saw it at the same time that Maya did. "It's another trick! Another empty house!"

Maya went over to the postcard, picking it up and looking it over. The front had a slightly strange bunny motif this time, with the usual cartoon bunnies apparently engaged in some kind of grand search. One was reading a map, another had out a compass. One seemed to be doing a math problem as it took sightings from the stars. A couple had stopwatches that they seemed to be comparing.

On the back, the writing was brief and to the point.

Clues get clues, not bunnies.

"You're right," Maya said to her boss. "There's no woman here. It says that clues get clues, not bunnies."

"Then this is over." Harris said. "This is the problem with trying to humor the dangerous crazies, Grey. They do what they want. They don't keep their end of the deal. Of *course* he was going to make us run around and then not give us anything. He gave you some help with this? So in his head the deal is square?"

163

"I'm not sure that's what it means, sir," Maya said.

It didn't fit with what she'd seen of the Moonlight Killer so far. Yes, he liked to play games, but there was a strange element of fairness to them. There was always a chance to win, as if a foregone conclusion simply wasn't interesting to him. He liked to hide things too, liked to have layers of understanding to show how clever he was.

"Then what else does it mean?" Harris asked. "He's played you, Grey. Played us."

"I think he's playing *with* us," Maya said. "He said a clue for a clue. So what if this postcard is a clue to the *actual* location of his victim?"

She looked at all those bunnies on the front, searching frantically, in a mirror image of her own search. It could just be a cruel taunt, but Maya wanted to believe that they meant something more than that. She stared at them, and one thing occurred to her.

"There are numbers on here," she said. She showed Harris the postcard. "Look, all the different bunnies doing things, but so many of them involve numbers. There's one solving an equation. There are the ones with stopwatches, one looking at the stars to navigate..."

The idea of it hit her in a rush. When people navigated by the stars, they were looking for latitude and longitude, right? Was *that* what the Moonlight Killer was doing here?

"I think... I think that there are coordinates hidden here," Maya said. "But jumbled up, so that we have to work out what's what."

Harris looked surprised, but then nodded. "In that case, these two, 39 and -77, would be the degrees."

"Sir?"

"Those are the degrees of latitude and longitude for the area around Washington," Harris said, with the certainty of someone who had probably had to use them plenty of times to give exact locations to agents.

"Then we just need the minutes and seconds," Maya said. She realized then that the bunnies were essentially in two groups. One was closer to the one with the map, which had 39 written on it in place of an x. The other group was closer to one that was writing on a slate as it copied -77 from a signpost.

Two groups, dividing the coordinates. Maya looked for clocks and watches next. There were two bunnies with those. One had no hour hand, and the minute hand pointed to 11, while the other had the minute

164

hand pointing to nine and the hour hand at one. Maya guessed that meant 69.

As for the rest, Maya realized that the other bunnies in each group were arranged left to right, so what if that meant the numbers should just be read that way?

"Try 39 degrees 11 minutes 98.6074507095 seconds, -77 degrees 69 minutes 54.6211909548 seconds," Maya said, reading it off.

She saw Harris put the location into his phone.

"That's a location a little way west of DC," the deputy director said.

Maya knew they had it right then. Would it be her sister waiting this time? Either way, they had to get to the woman waiting there, before it was too late.

*

They sped out to the location on the map. It was open ground, with no sign of any buildings, yet Maya got out of the car anyway, wanting to check the space on foot.

"There's nothing here," Harris said. "We must have gotten it wrong. That, or the kidnapper is just playing another game."

Maya didn't believe that, though. This *had* to be right. She kept looking around the space near the coordinates, looking for anything that might be a spot where the Moonlight Killer might stash a victim.

Her eyes fell on an old well, crumbling and covered over. It was just about the only manmade structure out there.

She ran to it, tearing that cover off and peering down into it using a torch. It was hard to see anything for a second or two even like that, but then she saw eyes looking back at her, wide and terrified.

"Here!" she yelled. "There's a woman here!"

The rest of the team came running, even as Maya realized that the rope that would normally have led down to a bucket was in much better condition than the rest of the well. It was brand new, and looked more like climbing rope than anything that would normally have been used for something like this. The mechanism on the well looked newer than it should have, too. The Moonlight Killer had dangled his captive like a worm on a line, waiting to be hauled up.

Maya started to use that mechanism to haul the woman up, pulling her up towards safety. She had the impression of a frightened young woman, smaller than she was, bound up in a climbing harness with ropes until she couldn't move. How long had she been left like that?

"It's all right," Maya said. "You're safe now. What's your name?"

"Gabi... Gabi Dubov."

Maya had no time to ask the young woman more than that, because the EMTs with them were already rushing past her, pulling the young woman out of the well, cutting her free of the ropes and rushing her to the ambulance.

Harris was there beside Maya then, putting a hand on her shoulder.

"You did it, Grey. You saved her."

Maya hoped so. After what had happened last time, Maya wasn't going to let the young woman out of her sight until she was sure that she was safe.

CHAPTER THIRTY

For the third time in a week, Maya found herself standing outside a hospital room, waiting for answers. This time, though, there was a member of hospital security on the door, because it was obvious that the ER staff remembered what had happened the last time the FBI had been there.

There weren't as many of the FBI there this time, though, just Maya, waiting out in the corridor. After what had happened with the fake clue the Moonlight Killer had planted in Liza Carty's head, it was obvious that Harris wasn't as keen to jump on everything this latest victim said.

That meant Maya had to wait, pacing there out in the corridor, hoping that a doctor would eventually come to speak with her. So far, all she had was a name, and she was sure that Harris and the rest were already going through all the details of Gabi Dubov's life, trying to work out exactly when and where she'd been taken.

Of course, it might have helped them to know exactly who they were dealing with, but Maya still hadn't told them her theory yet. She was still too worried about how Harris might react. She knew that she shouldn't hold back relevant information, but she told herself that, so far, all she had was a supposition, based on who would want the case solved.

That was an excuse, though, and she knew it. It was a way of justifying something that she might have done even if she'd had cold, hard proof of the Moonlight Killer's involvement.

Maya was still pacing when a doctor came out of the room that they'd put Gabi Dubov in.

"As far as we can tell, Ms. Dubov is physically fine," he said. "She's exhausted and dehydrated, but all she really needs is rest. You won't be able to talk to her before the morning, though."

There was a definite note in that, and Maya guessed that the doctor had heard what had happened with Liza Carty.

"You're sure she's all right?" Maya asked. "There's no sign that anything might happen to her?"

"None," the doctor said.

Maya dared to breathe a sigh of relief. It meant that Liza Carty's death had been an accident, rather than the Moonlight Killer snatching her away after releasing her. It meant that if she kept solving these cases, there was a chance that the women he held might come out of this alive.

"All right," Maya said. "I'll come back in the morning. But I *will* need to speak to her then. There are still other women being held by the man who kidnapped her."

She left the hospital and got out her phone to call Harris. She needed to let him know what was happening. As she did so, though, a message on her phone caught Maya's eye. It told her to call the prison at Pollock as soon as possible.

Maya hadn't thought that she would hear anything more from the prison, except possibly at Ade Matheson's trial. She'd thought that she was done with the whole town, now that she'd solved the one big mystery that had touched it. Briefly, the thought came to her that she might have gotten something wrong; but no, the Moonlight Killer had given up Gabi Dubov. Even *he'd* agreed that she'd found the right answer.

What did it say about her life when Maya was looking to a serial killer for confirmation that she'd done things correctly?

She called the prison at the number from the message.

"Hello, this is Governor Hale, at Pollock Correctional Facility. Who is this?"

"Agent Grey, of the FBI. You messaged me?"

"Ah, Agent, yes, I'm afraid I have some bad news, and I thought you would want to know."

That didn't tell Maya anything, and all the possibilities started swirling in her head. Had Matheson recanted his confession? Was there a problem with J.D.'s release?

"What kind of bad news?" Maya asked.

"I regret to inform you that an inmate you visited, Ade Matheson, is dead."

"He's *dead*?"

That news caught Maya a little off guard. The serial killer had obviously been a tough, dangerous man, so how could he be dead? Had someone shanked him by surprise? Had the upgrade to serial killer that he'd boasted about painted a target on his back?

168

"He was found hanged in his cell earlier," the governor said. "He committed suicide."

"What? How? I thought dangerous prisoners were watched!" Maya said.

"It happened between rounds by the guards," the governor explained. "And unless a prisoner is considered a specific suicide risk, they are not denied simple bedsheets. With hindsight, we should have seen that having fresh crimes discovered would create an additional risk."

"No, that's not right," Maya said.

"I know this is a shock," the governor replied, "and obviously, we will review our systems to see if there is anything that we can do to prevent such a thing from happening again, but *right*? Frankly, I think that this is the only right thing Ade Matheson has ever done. Don't lose sleep over this, Agent Grey. I know no one here will be."

The governor hung up, leaving Maya alone with the thought that something was very wrong about all this.

It wasn't that Ade Matheson was a great loss to the world. He was a self-confessed serial killer who had reveled in what he'd done when Maya had found him out. He was never getting out of prison, and would probably have remained a danger to both the guards there and other inmates for as long as he lived. It wasn't even the sense that, despite all that, a human life was a precious enough thing that its loss was sad, or that Maya would have preferred Matheson to stand trial so that justice could be done.

It wasn't any of that. It was simply that she had a hard time believing that Ade Matheson might have hanged himself at all.

Suicide might have made sense to the governor, but only because the man hadn't seen Matheson in the interview room, hadn't heard his casual arrogance at being found out. A man who hanged himself after being found out did so out of guilt, or out of fear of the consequences later on. Neither of those things applied to Ade Matheson.

Instead, Matheson had been almost triumphant, throwing his crimes in Maya's face with the knowledge that nothing else could happen to him there. He'd talked about how becoming known as a serial killer would make him king of the yard. He'd thought that all of this made things *better* for him, not worse.

Could he suddenly have realized the downsides? Could he have started to understand how much harder his life was about to be now that

169

the guards thought that he'd murdered one of their own? It was possible, but Maya didn't buy it. Matheson had killed four guards. He must have known what would happen if he were ever found out. It wasn't something he was going to suddenly realize and then hang himself.

If Maya didn't believe that he'd done it himself, though, what did that leave? One possibility that it was revenge by the guards on a man who had killed so many of them in different prisons. Again, though, Maya wasn't sure that it fit the facts. The simple truth was that, as broken as J.D. was, he'd made it through his time in the prison without anything like this happening to him. If the guards were truly interested in revenge on Samantha Neele's killer, then surely he would have been dead before now too.

That left one possibility in Maya's mind: that somehow, the Moonlight Killer had found a way to get at Ade Matheson in prison. That he'd exacted his revenge for another serial killer's crimes being passed off as his.

It was a terrifying thought, because of what it said about the Moonlight Killer's ability to get at anyone, anywhere. If he could kill someone, or have them killed, in the middle of a crowded prison, that meant either that he was a ghost who could slip through any defense, or it meant that he had dangerous contacts who were willing to do whatever he asked.

Maya wasn't sure which possibility was more frightening. It was obvious that the Moonlight Killer was getting *some* help, wittingly or unwittingly, because of the postcards that kept showing up so quickly, and because of the level of surveillance he was obviously able to maintain. It was a big leap from that though to say that someone was prepared to kill for him.

Either way, it meant that Maya was locked in a dangerous game with a man who had skills and resources that could reach out to hurt her at any time. This was a man who had made twelve women disappear without a trace, a man who could trick and trap the FBI's finest whenever they tried to hunt him down.

Thinking of all that, it was hard not to be afraid.

Fear wasn't going to stop Maya from doing her job, though. Tomorrow, she would arrange to go back to Pollock even though she had been determined never to set foot in the place again. She would go to the prison, and she would find out exactly what had happened there.

170

Maybe it would give her information that would lead her to the Moonlight Killer, and to her sister.

At the very least, it might shed some light on what the goal was with this grand game of his. Did he really just want to set the record straight about who had committed which crimes, or was there more to it than that?

Maya was still trying to make sense of it when her phone rang. It was Harris.

"Grey, I have news for you."

"That Ade Matheson is dead?"

"What?"

Apparently, no one had told the deputy director yet.

"I just had a call from the prison, saying that he'd been hanged."

"He killed himself?" It was obvious from Harris' tone that he didn't think it was a bad thing. Probably he was thinking about all the time and trouble it would save with no need for a trial.

"That's what they're saying," Maya said. "I'm not sure if I believe it."

She realized that if she said more than that, she might have to give away her suspicions about the kidnapper. It seemed better to deflect the conversation in another direction.

"What's your news, sir, if it's not about Matheson?"

"We finally got the forensics on the hair that came with the photographs," Harris said. "There's no easy way to say this, Grey. It's from your sister."

Maya felt dizzy then. She'd known that Megan was there with the kidnapper from the moment she received the postcard with her handwriting, but this was definitive proof. It was more than that, too.

Had Megan been the one in those photographs? Had she been the one the Moonlight Killer had hurt so systematically, just to make a point to the FBI about not trying to find him. The thought of that made Maya angry and terrified for her sister all at once.

Her sister might be sitting in a room somewhere, bruised and bloodied, because of her department. She would be frightened, knowing that at any moment her captor might try to hurt her more, or even kill her.

Now that Maya knew who that captor was, she was even more afraid. If this had been some strange vigilante trying to catch the Moonlight Killer, there would have still been danger, but Maya might

171

have had some confidence that ultimately, she would get her sister back if she just went along with everything.

Instead, Megan was in the hands of a deadly serial killer, one who struck and left no traces, one who the collective efforts of the FBI hadn't been able to find. Both she and Maya were caught in the Moonlight Killer's web, and Maya couldn't see a good way out, for either of them.

The only thing she could do was wait for the next postcard.

And hope that this time, she would have enough information to find her sister.

NOW AVAILABLE!

GIRL THREE: TRAPPED
(A Maya Gray FBI Suspense Thriller —Book 3)

12 cold cases. 12 kidnapped women. One diabolical serial killer. In this riveting suspense thriller, a brilliant FBI agent faces a deadly challenge: decipher the mystery before each one is murdered.

In the Maya Gray series (which begins with Book #1—GIRL ONE: MURDER) FBI Special Agent Maya Gray, 39, has seen it all. She's one of BAU's rising stars and the go-to agent for hard-to-crack serial cases. When she receives a handwritten postcard promising to release 12 kidnapped women if she will solve 12 cold cases, she assumes it's a hoax.

Until the note mentions that, among the captives, is her missing sister.

Maya, shaken, is forced to take it seriously. The cases she's up against are some of the most difficult the FBI has ever seen. But the terms of his game are simple: If Maya solves a case, he will release one of the girls.

And if she fails, he will end a life.

In GIRL THREE: TRAPPED (book #3), case three has just landed, and the clock is ticking. The suspect, a copycat of the Moonlight Killer, seems to be using sophisticated audio equipment to stay one step ahead of his victims—and Maya herself could be next.

Maya, knowing the killer has her sister, has no choice but to accept the case. More determined than ever, she revisits the prison where the last convict hung himself in hopes of uncovering a new lead. But with the murderer able to track her every movement, Maya realizes that she's the least safe of all.

And in the midst of it all, a bunny escapes.

A complex psychological crime thriller full of twists and turns and packed with heart-pounding suspense, the MAYA GRAY mystery series will make you fall in love with a brilliant new female protagonist and keep you turning pages late into the night. It is a perfect addition for fans of Robert Dugoni, Rachel Caine, Melinda Leigh or Mary Burton.

Future books in the series will be available soon.

Molly Black

Debut author Molly Black is author of the MAYA GRAY FBI suspense thriller series, comprising six books (and counting); and the RYLIE WOLF FBI suspense thriller series, comprising three books (and counting).

An avid reader and lifelong fan of the mystery and thriller genres, Molly loves to hear from you, so please feel free to visit www.mollyblackauthor.com to learn more and stay in touch.

BOOKS BY MOLLY BLACK

MAYA GRAY FBI SUSPENSE THRILLER
GIRL ONE: MURDER (Book #1)
GIRL TWO: TAKEN (Book #2)
GIRL THREE: TRAPPED (Book #3)
GIRL FOUR: LURED (Book #4)
GIRL FIVE: BOUND (Book #5)
GIRL SIX: FORSAKEN (Book #6)

RYLIE WOLF FBI SUSPENSE THRILLER
FOUND YOU (Book #1)
CAUGHT YOU (Book #2)
SEE YOU (Book #3)

Lightning Source UK Ltd.
Milton Keynes UK
UKHW010253090223
416650UK00002B/412